Testament

Richard W. Kelly

Testament

TITLES BY RICHARD W. KELLY
MEENDUK.COM

Bizarro
- The Cattercorns of Cloudville Arizona

Christian
- My Journey Into Christianity
- Noel Not an Angel: A Christmas Novella

Fantasy
- Kings of One Color

Historical Fiction
- The Early Years of 'Squirt' Malone

Horror
- Testament

Short Stories
- Solundrums
- Solundrums V.2

Slice of Life Books
- The Cultural Phenomenon of Super Jam and the Tragedy Therein
- Lost Vegas, Nevada
- A Novella About Pie That Should Have Starred Jason Sudeikis
- Times… They Are A Changin'

Thriller
- The American Martyr
- The MARX Beasts

Young Adult
- The Psi-Chotic Adventures of Drew Darby

THANK YOU

To everyone who supported me in my early attempts at writing. I'm including everyone! My parents, my sister, my grandparents, my wife, my kids, my writing teacher in fourth grade, my creative writing teacher in eleventh grade, my guitar teacher, my philosophy teacher, my friends from high school, my friends after high school, the few people in the dorm in college who read my stuff and critiqued me, extended family, professional authors that had words of encouragement, and anyone else that I may be forgetting.

The Daily Examiner

Last night there was a double murder during a possible robbery at a gas station on Melor Avenue. Two male victims were fatally shot. The clerk of the establishment was missing upon the arrival of law enforcement. The police claim to have a lead on the possible killer.

Thomas Year 0 Day 0

Buzzing sounds filled the air. Thomas rolled over in his queen-sized bed, flinging his hand in the process. His palm slammed down on the alarm clock, silencing his room for the next few minutes thanks to the snooze button. In the back of his head, he knew he had to get up, but it was no use. Responsibility was not going to win out over comfort. Instead, he snuggled his head against his time-flattened pillow. If it were not for the garbage truck slamming his apartment's dumpster into the ground, Thomas may not have got up at all that day. Instead, he started on a path that would change the world.

The loud bang of the dumpster caused Thomas to eject himself from his comfortable cuddle to a stiff, upright position. The shock left him out of breath and slightly nervous in his own darkened bedroom. He got to his knees so he could crawl out of bed. His dingy hair hung in his face, leaving a partially obscured view.

He scuttled off the plush mattress to a standing position on the floor. The dirt ingrained in his typical apartment brown carpet pressed against his feet, reminding him of just how high class he was not. Thomas reached down and swiped his work shirt and black denim pants from the sullied floor while forcing his mind to come to grips with the fact that he was going to have to go to work.

He peeked around the corner into the bathroom. A shower should have been necessary, but he kept walking. His refusal to bathe was not driven by the mold on the walls, the lack of soap, or the already-dripping faucet. It was pure laziness of not wanting to shower.

Thomas pulled his shirt over his head as he walked into the kitchen. The roaches scattered as the cabinet opened and he blindly reached in for his puffed rice cereal. The bright white refrigerator stood out in the kitchen. It was the only thing in the room that did not look like it had been blasted with dirt. His former fridge had gone out months ago and the landlord had finally replaced it last week.

He pulled open the door of the new white machine and yanked out the milk. With a quick glance, he noticed it was two weeks past the expiration and tossed the whole carton into the sink. The slime in the unclean bowl caused the milk carton to slide around as if it were a basketball rolling around the edge of the hoop.

Thomas reached his hand into the cereal box and

pulled out his breakfast. With his free hand, he maneuvered his pants up his legs, unfortunately, dropping some rice puffs on the floor, adding to the filth of the apartment. The bare walls watched as Thomas slipped his shoes on, finished his handful of cereal, and headed toward the door to walk to work. As his hand grasped the cold brass doorknob, a buzzing suddenly came from his bedroom.

Thomas sprinted the six feet back into his room to turn off his alarm clock. As he slid the switch to the left, a small shimmer from the barrel of his pistol caught his eye. The gun was quickly tucked into his waistband. Almost forgot my bodyguard, he thought. It was the only attention he paid the weapon at the time, even though it would change his day … and his life. He patted his pockets to make sure he did not forget anything else: keys, gum, money, wallet. Everything was ready.

The late-afternoon sun nearly blinded Thomas as he walked out of his cave of a dwelling. Working nights led him to believe blacking out all his windows was a necessity, but in reality, it did nothing more than help him sleep through his alarm. He walked out of the parking lot of his complex and onto the sidewalk. The familiar scent of exhaust wafted by Thomas as he robotically began to make his two-mile walk to work.

As usual, he passed by a couple of bums, a lot of graffiti, and a few morally questionable activities, but these images did not even catch his eye. His mind skipped over the decay of the city because his daily routine of walking to work was a time to reminisce. He was otherwise rarely self-reflective, but there was something about walking around town by himself that just forced his mind to wander to the familiar.

He was ten years out of high school and this was not where he had pictured himself. Back then, it was nothing but ideas of success. He thought he might even own a business one day, getting up day after day, drumming up clients like his father. This type of dream would have required a lot of work on his part over the previous decade and he was not that dedicated.

He only lasted one semester in junior college. The temptations were too much. How could he force himself to go off to class every day when he did not have to? If he could have seen his punctuality issues in awaking for his current job, he would have known the foregone conclusion. He often wondered if he should return to higher education, but he always shot the thought down before it got too far. It was not that he did not want a better life. It was that he was a lazy man who was afraid of failure.

"Don't walk" sign. Thomas leaned up against the traffic light, still squinting from the now-fading sunlight. Why can't it always be midnight? Thomas thought as the walk sign flickered. He checked to see if any cars were coming, as that side of town had a tendency to not adhere to traffic laws. He clicked his heels on the uneven asphalt that covered the road as he journeyed toward his place of employment.

Upon his return to the sidewalk, he passed by a

woman dragging her small son. The boy was taking wobbling steps while his mother held his hand straight above his head, barely allowing him to reach the litter-covered ground with each short stride.

He wondered if there had ever been a time when his parents helped him along in such a way. The only memories he had of his parents were when he dropped out of college, there was a lot of disappointment, shouting, and ultimatums. He understood it was his own fault and he needed to "grow up," as they say, but he was holding a grudge he could not let go. He felt there was an indoctrination of his mind from a small age. He construed his parents' constant encouragement as a forced destiny to attend a university and earn a degree. This morbid view of the love and support he received was just the beginning of his twisted self-image as the black sheep of the family.

In reality, his parents, just like all parents, were proud of him. They wished he had finished his schooling, but there was no chance that they would ever be ashamed of their son. They truly felt that he was lost. That they somehow misguided him, but they loved him, of that there was no doubt. They made mistakes.

The day he told them he was no longer attending school, there were comparisons to his brothers, there was some shouting, and worst of all, there was an empty threat. Unfortunately, Thomas misread that threat and he left. It was the end of that relationship. The lack of the nurturing environment needed to help him grow into the logical mind-set was a fatal blow to their family unit.

Thomas walked by the topless club that he frequented. The neon lights buzzed slightly as he walked past, breaking his concentration on his parents. As he passed by the establishment, he wondered if he would ever think of his parents if it were not for the daily walks to work.

He looked back over his shoulder to get a last look at the club. The closest people in his life over the last couple of years were his regular dancers. Other than them, his television was the only other thing that had any glimpse into Thomas's life. His lack of friends and lack of female companionship made the topless club an ideal hangout for the young man. That was his first reason for going.

The obsession eventually grew into Thomas's habits, as did everything he fixated his mind on. There was an odd addiction mentality that flowed through the young man, every activity he enjoyed would become a recurring endeavor. Just hammer the same thing until he eventually lost interest. It had been this way from his life as a small child, collecting baseball cards, playing video games, watching TV. It, of course, hardened into a more devastating habit as he aged, allowing him to be exploited by strippers, alcohol, and the casino's when he came into a state that housed some.

Over halfway to work, he thought about some of the dancers he had met there over the years. Desire, Chastity, Pleasure, Peach ... He was sure they were all on to bigger and better things by now. Would they even remember him at this point? He shook the thought from his head. He did not want to deal with the reality that he was nothing more than a paycheck to those girls. At least he was not losing his money to that wannabe bordello any more.

There was a loud echoing bang that came from behind Thomas. Fearing it was a gunshot he turned back while ducking behind a mailbox. He had his hand under his shirt, gripping the handle of his pistol, ready to draw the weapon if need be. His respiratory rate had begun to quicken, and his eyes were darting back and forth looking for the life-altering event. There was no sign of anything. The left side of the street was completely empty and the right side consisted of a couple of squirrels playing with the garbage debris, the typical infestation of the sidewalks.

Assuming it was a car backfire, he resumed his walk to work. These types of reaction were par for the area he lived in. Although it was a concern he dealt with on a normal occasion and he should have been used to it, he could not keep the possibility of a gunshot out of his head. The security policy in waistband always helped him feel safe, but the fact that it was illegal for him to possess always left him on edge. But, living on the bad side of town made owning the gun a better bet than not.

Thomas always said, "It's better to be alive in prison than dead and law-abiding." Of course, he could have bought it legally and registered himself with the authorities, but spending that kind of cash would have bankrupted him for months and caused him more work than he cared to contend with.

He rounded the final corner of his journey. The sun now setting created a bright haze over the gas station where Thomas worked. The gas pumps painted with graffiti and clad in cracked glass appeared to wave in the heat, looking as though they were part of a dying sauna. The location of the store always perplexed Thomas. It was on a minor street hidden by two large buildings on either side of it. It was set far enough back from the street itself that you had to know it was there or you would always pass it on the first go.

He went inside and exchanged pleasantries with the outgoing employee, switching the cash drawers and speaking about the issues of the day. Once the other employee was gone, Thomas removed his gun from his waistband and placed it under the counter where he had access to it at all times.

His shift was to consist of checking people out, cleaning the store, and helping customers in any way they needed. For the most part, Thomas only operated the cash register. He was not concerned with customer satisfaction or the cleanliness of the store itself. In fact, he was constantly playing two games in his head.

The first was a counting game where he would see how many times a customer would ask for help before they decided he was either deaf or rude. This game commonly caused many people to walk out without buying anything, but that never weighed on Thomas's decision to play.

The second was a guessing game that centered on trying to see how much dust and dirt could collect around each customer. He had a person at one point that literally had a dust bunny that covered his entire shoe. This game almost felt like watching art.

Each person would walk into the store, causing a disruption in the dirt colony on the floor. A little tornado of grime would circle their feet as they moved to a shelf to look for their specific item. As they would pick up different products, dust would fall off them and onto the floor, intermingling with the muck already there.

Seeing these little drops fall into a bigger ocean of dirt was very serene and always left Thomas pondering the bigger picture. It was almost a metaphor for his life and how each disturbing issue would build, creating who he was, his own ocean of filth.

This is how he spent his night, hour after hour of painful, slow monotony until two o'clock in the morning. It had been over ten minutes since Thomas had a customer come in the store. He was lost in nonthought staring, gazing aimlessly at the Styrofoam-tiled drop ceiling. Just when he was about to start counting the miniature holes in each tile, a couple of men cautiously sauntered into the store.

The Daily Examiner

After the early shooting Thursday morning, the attendant for the local gas station is still missing. The situation has been filed as a missing person's case. Although the police will not comment, the aforementioned missing person may be a suspect in the shooting.

Thomas Year 0 Day 1 AV

Thomas lost his focus on the insignificant ceiling and watched the men as they quickly went to the back of the store. Their behavior was off-putting, to say the least. One of the men, tall and lanky, was grabbing things off the shelf while staring out the window. His dark eyes were constantly darting left and right, as if he were on the lookout for something while his dirty-blond hair swayed in the opposite direction of his eyes in large chunks held together by the man's obvious refusal to wash it. The other man was much shorter than his partner or Thomas. He sported a brown leather biker jacket and enough tattoos to warrant a commission for the advertising he gave the artist. He stared directly at Thomas, not trying to hide his gaze in any way.

This put Thomas on high alert. Standing behind the counter, he put his hand on his gun, just in case. Sweat beaded over his brow as his pointer finger caressed the trigger of his weapon. After a short amount of time, the tall man, still looking out the window, was holding a large amount of potato chips, tampons, and motor oil. It was obvious he had no idea what had ended up in his arms. The short man, still staring at Thomas, tapped the tall man on the arm and began swiftly walking toward the cash register.

As the men were moving toward Thomas, his brain started working faster than his body could handle. He grasped the handle of the firearm tightly as he recalled his list of reasons why it was safe to work at a gas station overnight. All of those reasons he created months ago seemed to not be sensible now, realizing his current situation. As the two men approached, he felt worried and lonely.

The short man having reached the counter shouted at Thomas, "Give me all the money in the register!"

Thomas was in shock. He could not move. His body stood there frozen with one hand beneath the counter holding onto his weapon, the other flat on the counter not moving toward the money like the robbers desired. The tall man, still walking toward the counter, said with an odd Southern accent, "Look at his arm. He's hittin' an alarm, or he's got a gun."

Thomas's body went into automatic pilot. The leather-clad intruder started to pull out a weapon of his own, while Thomas's trigger finger instinctively pulled back. It was an odd feeling. Thomas pulled the trigger three times in short succession, firing bullets through the counter itself. The man's body twisted and turned as the bullets made plywood splinters chaotically fly through the air just before they traveled through his body. The gangly man fumbled with his gun as he began to shoot before he had aimed in Thomas's direction.

It could have been the fear of being shot or the realization that he may have just killed someone, but Thomas collapsed to the ground, still clinging to his weapon. He landed hard on the floor behind the counter with his head slamming into the concrete. In the fetal position, his head bounced up and then hit the ground a second time in rebound from the hard fall. The jarring of his brain inside his skull caused the light in the room to hurt his eyes momentarily, but he was relieved to be alive, until he noticed the tall man standing over him, pointing his gun in Thomas's face.

The tall man shook slightly. The gun gently clicked as his hand shivered side to side. They both looked back at the other robber shot dead, motionless on the ground. Slowly, they moved their gazes back toward each other.

The living robber aimed his gun at Thomas's head and tried to swallow the massive amount of saliva that was building up in his mouth. His tongue scraped across his dry lips. As soon as Thomas saw the man's index finger extend and start to pull back, his body returned to autopilot.

His life did not flash before his eyes. There was no intimidation from the gun being aimed at his head, just mechanical reactions to a traumatic experience. Before the awkward man could build the gall to avenge the death of his partner, Thomas twisted his hand to point his weapon upward and pulled the trigger twice. His body had every intention of shooting again, but the splatter of blood on his face disturbed his plans.

There was a dull thump as the robber fell backwards onto the dirty floor and Thomas went limp. He lay there quiet and still for an inordinate amount of time. The realization that he had just taken two lives was a revelation that was lingering around the corner, then there was nothing but relief in that room. The adrenaline in his body seemed to ooze out of his ears, down the side of his head, and all over the floor.

The idea of calling 911 crossed his mind, but he could barely force himself to think, much less move his body. Staring up at the ceiling, Thomas realized how relaxing the world could be. Moments before, there was pandemonium in his place of work, but after the necessary events transpired, there was a perfect calm. The only motion in the entire building was his heartbeat.

He could have remained there relaxed forever, but a loud bang disrupted the ambiance as the front door forcibly flew open, slamming into the counter. Thomas could feel the presence of something dark, a sinister yet stealthy being which glided throughout the store. It stopped at Thomas's feet. The creature moved gracefully as it lightly traced his arm with its fingers. Still looking straight ahead at the ceiling, Thomas found himself unable to breathe. Panic was setting in and it left him immobile, frozen in terror.

The dark and silky hair of the thing swayed into

Thomas's view. It was the smoothest and finest looking mane he had ever seen, conjuring up memories of chinchillas and rabbits he had as a child. Then unexpectedly, a severe pain immediately followed the image.

His neck was being crushed by something razor sharp. Thomas could feel his esophagus collapsing under the pressure of what his mind rationalized to be a bear trap. The anguish snapped him out of his statuesque state, gasping for air and shooting to a sit.

He tried to inhale. It did nothing but force pressure in his chest, which was trying to collapse in on itself from the closed airway in his gullet. The being jumped back so dramatically that it hit the ceiling, its head crashing through a Styrofoam panel. Its eyes focused on Thomas and infected the rest of his face with a look of sheer panic.

Thomas, not being overly observant while he was convinced of his impending death, only got a quick glimpse of his attacker. It was a tall, slender man who was nearly as pale as the fluorescent lights illuminating the store. The thing that would have haunted Thomas's dreams was the fact that the man had a mouth full of blood, his blood, which was wide open in its frightened capacity while Thomas continued to struggle for air.

The man quickly dashed out of the store and out into the street, leaving Thomas to suffer.

It was at that moment Thomas wished for death. He was losing consciousness from lack of oxygen and his throat was in unbearable pain. He could feel the warmth of his blood pouring out his neck and onto his shirt, leaving him bathing in his own life-source. His eyes darted left and right, looking for something to stop the pain, but he had no idea what to do. He could not speak, he could not breathe, he could barely move.

The fear surged a second wind of energy he used to look down at his body. Lying flat on the floor, he could see the color fading from his skin. The sight brought horror to his mind as he could not fathom he was losing blood that quickly.

He knew it must be his imagination, but he could hear a sizzling sound as his pigment fled his skin. He focused on his hands, watching as a release of his tincture took place as if a volume of water were slowly making its way toward his fingertips. As soon as his hands were a bloodless pale, he felt the burning move into his eyes.

He shoved his palms into his eye sockets, trying to push the pain back down the ocular nerves. All sounds around him were intensifying. The wounds in his neck began to throb. The pulsation of his injuries became so intense that the skin felt as though it were stretching and tightening around his neck.

Realizing how long it had been since he could breathe, he tried to force some air through his lungs. It was to no avail, but for some reason, he did not feel as though it were a necessity anymore. His body seemed to function and grow slightly stronger, even without oxygen. He subliminally questioned his sanity, assuming the lack of air was driving him off the deep end and into a pool of hallucination and irrationality.

His body started to go cold, but as his body heat evaporated, he felt his liveliness return. In fear of his physical injuries, he did not want to move, but all of his muscles tensed up, ready for action.

There comes a point in many people's lives where they feel they have left reality. This experience was no different. Lost somewhere between sleep and consciousness, his entire body was numb, leaving his pain past tense. Breathing had become a phantom of his brain. He knew he had to be inhaling, but there was no proof that it was happening.

Reaching for his throat, trying to find something to ground him in reality, he found no wounds. His lack of injury was incomprehensible. He was just bit in the throat by some vicious being and moments later, he was sitting on the floor with no pain, no bleeding, and no injuries.

His mind retreated and let him fall into a fantasy, a daydream. There was nothing to bring him back. His body sat on the floor of the gas station while his mind trekked through his life. He tried to force the life flashing before his eyes to happen. He remembered his childhood, his romances, his family. He attempted everything to allow himself to pass on. He craved his ascension to the afterlife, but all he got was tunnel vision and a washing out of colors as his eyes seemed to become more susceptible to the light.

Forcing himself to move, he reached a kneeling

position, trying to get to his feet. Having received such a shock to his psyche, he did not know if he was in the real world or a dream state, but his perception of the world was suddenly much more vibrant. The dark and dingy place that he called work had new life inside of it. The grays of the floor seemed to dance with the yellows of the counters almost visibly mixing before his eyes. It was a psychedelic animation that seemed to belong in an acid trip. He quickly turned his head to the side and nearly fell to the ground as the earthy tones of the sandwiches attacked his vision like a spotlight in the face.

Looking down, Thomas saw the two corpses of his previous attackers lying motionless on the floor, reminding him of the possibility that he may have lost his mind. Could he possibly have murdered the two men and envisioned the being attacking him? Had the act of taking a life sent him over the edge and forced him to become a self-delusional killer?

Still staring off at the dead bodies, he noticed that his hand was clutching the murder weapon. There was no chance he was getting out of this one, not in the liberal town he lived in, there murder was murder. He knew he was in possession of an illegal firearm. He stared down at the dead robbers, feeling a lump build in his throat. It was a lump of fear, of sorrow, of sadness for what he had been forced to give up. His gaze, trained on the dead men, kept his entire body in check until the door opened.

Thomas immediately looked up to see a man running frantically down the street away from the gas station. He had obviously seen the two dead robbers and Thomas standing over them with his gun. Did he flee for his life or to fetch the police? Thomas may not have the luxury of turning himself in anymore. He could be reported before he could convince himself to even lift the phone and call the authorities.

He walked over to the register and pressed three of the glossy buttons to get the cash drawer open. All the money not in the safe went into his pockets, along with the gun. He leapt over the counter and went out the door into the city. He had no idea where he was going, but he knew he needed to run if he did not want to spend the rest of his life behind bars. He began sprinting full speed down the street and somehow began to relax as he watched the scenery blend together as the colors in his sight swirled around to make one blob of color.

It was a tunnel of colors. The pallet of the world mingled with itself, creating a rainbow-painted tube that Thomas was sprinting through. He was running down the street, taking corners at full speed, dodging the occasional pedestrian. There was nothing behind him that could convince him to go back to. There was a new life in front of him that he was rushing to reach. Behind him were his fears, his life as he had never wanted it to develop. All of his failures and broken dreams lingered back there and he had no intention to return.

His failure at education, his family failures, his career failures, his romantic failures, even his social failures were all topped off by the shooting of the two intruders at the gas station where he worked. The road in front of him was unknown and frightening, but the two dead bodies made sure he did not turn back. His mind clawed at ideas of what would happen if he were caught as his feet continued to race down the sidewalks of his hometown, ignoring his brain's temptations to stop. Would he go to jail? Would he be put to death? There would be no mercy if he were found. He was not the upper crust of society and would not be given a get-out-of-jail-free card.

Scenarios began to play out in his head as he turned a corner at full speed. Instantly, he stopped dead in his tracks, worried that the life behind him and the life in front of him may be one and the same. The blurring of his tunnel vision faded as the red brick buildings all came back into focus with a police car in the center of his view. Thankful that the cops had not looked his direction, he glanced to both sides in desperation for a place to hide.

The typical scene of urban society at four in the morning left little to conceal his person. He turned back around, facing the alley that he had just run down and slowly walked back toward the shadows in a valiant attempt at remaining inconspicuous.

It was nerve-racking for him to stroll back away from the police. Without being able to see them, he did not know if he was getting away. Had they found out about his murders yet? Were they watching him? All he could hope for was that it had not been reported yet. They would find out, there was no doubt about it. He did not even take the time to cover up his prints or mask his identity in any way. He had just run.

Once he knew he was out of the streetlights, he took off running again. He restricted himself to the back alleys. The direct routes of the major roads were not worth the risk of getting caught, especially when he had no destination. Moving faster than he ever thought possible, he bounded over dumpsters, animals, and other obstacles in his path. Having spent his entire life in the city, he knew every nook and cranny like the back of his hand. It took no thought, he just ducked in between buildings, down small streets, and through people's yards, not sure of where he was headed.

Dashing down a familiar road he thought he heard something chasing him. He tried to turn his head to look behind him, but his speed forced him to return his concentration forward. The fear that there might be an officer hunting him down, determined to put him behind bars fogged his judgment. He turned into an apartment parking lot and weaved through the parked cars, hoping to lose whoever was following.

Fence. He was trapped in a corner of the lot. He turned back and still did not see anyone or anything, just reigniting his fear that he may be losing his mind. There were a lot of cars nicely parked in the grid fashion the paint suggested in front of him and a fifteen-foot fence behind him. The sounds of the city seemed to fill his ears, screaming, honking, screeching, and sirens were all very audible to him. It was the sirens that made him resume his sprint.

He turned toward the massive fence and jumped

straight up, hoping against hope that he might be able to reach the top. His muscles contracted tighter than his body had ever felt as he pushed off the ground with a massive force from his calves. He startled himself as his feet cleared the fence and he fell the fifteen feet to the cement on the other side. He hit the ground hard, landing on a knee, feeling an immediate swelling of the joint. It could have been the adrenaline, but there was no pain from the landing, no strain from the jump, and no time to ponder these issues. He was off at full speed again.

He had been running for longer than he could keep track of when he realized there was no fatigue. He was as calm and relaxed as he would be after a long night's sleep. He was not panting, his pulse was not pounding, and he still had it in him to keep going. It was similar to a dream, when he would realize after hours of sleep that his dreams were impossible and that he was not in reality. But this time, he could not awake. He was conscious and this was not a delusion.

Time stood still as Thomas darted all over town. He eventually stopped at the center of the town square before the humongous yet beautifully built courthouse that looked down over the rest of the buildings in the square. Although he could not remember the connection he made, it was the sight of that building that brought him to the realization that he had been attacked by something inhuman. He could not put his finger on what it was, but he knew that it was not natural. Could it have been supernatural? A ghost? A god? A monster? A demon? There was no telling, but whatever it had been, it was having strange effects on his body.

Though he was not tired, he knew that he had expended an insurmountable amount of energy and he must need food. Turning away from the courthouse, he scanned the businesses in the square, hoping for a fast-food restaurant with an all-night dining room. The row of businesses in front of Thomas were all closed, as were the ones to his right, but a light was on in a burger joint to his left. Instinctively putting one foot in front of the other, his mind began to worry that he looked like he had been running from the police. He may not have felt worn-out, but his appearance might show it.

The door flung open with the slightest push from Thomas and the unbearably bright lights accompanied with the off-white and yellow décor reminded him of his gas station. There was the same feel of human desperation, the same horror of the real world, a personified version of everything he hated about his own life. On top of the depravity of the business itself was a stench of burning animal flesh that nearly nauseated Thomas.

Fearing that he looked like a fugitive on the run, Thomas turned right immediately upon entering the building to make a beeline to the restrooms. Throwing open the bathroom door, he was welcomed by a mirror with an odd reflection. He could tell he was looking at an image of himself, but it looked as though he were half-invisible. He could almost see through his body to the tiles on the wall. He was paler than he had ever thought a person could be, his eyes having lost all of their pigment, his hair stringy yet sleek. His veins were all beginning to become more visible through his skin, and the splatter of the robber's blood was still sprayed across his face.

He turned on the water and quickly rinsed his face, but his reflection remained cadaverous. He put his hands on the wet granite counter, trying to gather his bearings. Leaning forward, staring blankly into the sink, he again questioned his sanity. It was too much. Everything that night had become too weird, too surreal. No matter what thought he had, nothing made sense. Was he comatose and this was all a dream as he lay on the floor of the gas station? Maybe he had been drugged sometime that day and he was running around making a fool of himself while living a delusion. He could not convince himself of any scenario. The only thing he knew for sure was the stench of burning flesh lingered in the bathroom also.

He shook his head to refocus on the mission he had set for himself. Emerging from the bathroom, he looked over at the counter and began to stare at the girl behind it. Tall and slender, the girl looked back at Thomas. Her physical features were almost blank to him, but there was a bright glow and slight pulsation all around her body. He stared at her, seeing energy palpitate throughout her veins, looking like nothing he had seen before. It created a hazy movement similar to heat on a highway in the desert.

As he approached the counter, her features became clearer, but looking over her soft skin, his mind forcibly started to think about the girl's mood and emotions. Instinctively, he knew that she was intrigued by him, his look, his movements, and his intensity, which was focused solely on her at that moment.

The young girl, excited to speak to the mysterious customer, looked up at his face and asked what he would like to order. A smile shone through on her face as Thomas mentioned her beauty in contrast to the darkness of night. He ordered a hamburger after a couple of flirtatious smiles and comments. The girl was flustered but managed to get his burger from the back and gave it to him while she blushed from his suave demeanor.

He took the burger and walked to an open chair. He could not figure out what had come over him. He did not normally have the confidence to flirt with girls he did not know. It was a surprise he could be so charming. Her reaction reminded him of the strip club with the dancers clamoring around him as if he were their knight in shining armor. Of course, he always knew it was the money, but not with this girl. She could not have cared less if he were spending money at the burger joint.

Thomas looked down at the hamburger he had ordered and it appeared to be one of the least appetizing meals he had ever placed in front of himself. It was an experience he had never felt before. There were times in the past when meat was unappealing when he dwelled on it being a former mammal, there were times when things were repulsive because he just was not in the mood, but this time, it was as if someone had served him mud. Not as if he were uninterested, but almost as if it were not even food. He forced a few bites, but the majority of the burger joined the rest of the restaurant's waste in the garbage can.

He gave a quick wave and wink to the girl behind the counter as he walked back out into the city. In the open air, he looked up. He was not looking at buildings or people, he was looking at the night itself. There was a majestic quality that had previously gone unnoticed. The moon sat guard over the millions of stars throughout the sky as if it were a sheepdog watching over the flock. Seeing the contrast of distant objects pressed against the velvety black of night created a feeling of captivation within Thomas's soul. It was only the cool night breeze that helped drift Thomas's attention away from the infinite space of the universe back to the world he was standing upon.

Looking back to Earth, he noticed a few people wandering the streets at the late hour he was out. But just like with the girl behind the counter, he did not see specific features. Instead, he saw incredible glows and energy flowing through their veins. The pulsations of each different person showed the amazing dance of nature, the impossibility of everyone living in this world with overly complex biological systems.

As each person came closer to Thomas's location, he saw more of their personal glow. He could see their mood and sense their emotions. Bright blues, reds, and yellows bombarded his vision while the thoughts and worries of those people invaded his mind. He heard the screams and pleas of people he did not know, desiring everything from sexual gratification to large sums of money. He was not creating these thoughts, they were invading his mind.

Just like the night sky, his people-watching activity was quickly becoming a fascination. He lost track of time as he stared at passersby throughout the night, but he did notice the sun coming up. The light was barely peeking over the buildings when he felt a strange terror. The small amounts of light caused Thomas's vision to blend into a big pool of colors. His focus fell out of his control and his body was beginning to have trouble staying upright. He was weakening at an astonishing rate, feeling as if he had not slept in days and his body would not have it any more.

Thomas stumbled across the street and into the presence of the courthouse. As he stepped into the shade of the massive building, he began to feel a slight bit better. Feeling the tiny bit of relief, he collapsed on the lawn before the courthouse. However, it was only a temporary reprieve. As the sunlight got brighter, Thomas had more trouble seeing and began to feel vomit rise in his throat. The light appeared to attack all of his physical capacities as he began to feel a hint of pain on his skin.

He stood up and fumbled his way down the lane, looking for a place to rest. Being so early in the morning, nothing had opened yet. He began to head toward the burger place that he went to earlier that night, but before he could get to the door, he collapsed in the street, a burning rising up from the inside of his body. If it were not for the slanted roads and the rain gutter he slid into, he may have lay there all day in the punishing light. He slammed face-first into the concrete floor of the rain gutter, but he could already tell the pain was subsiding a bit.

The thud echoed throughout the modern-day bunker as Thomas's skull bounced off the paved floor. It was a relief to land in the shade, credit due to the engineer who designed the runoff-gutter system. The tension in his muscles relaxed as the cool morning breeze made its way into the small lateral portal from the outside world, whirling in the small room, creating invisible cyclones and other psychedelic patterns as it danced around the floor and across Thomas's limp, slowly rejuvenating body.

He looked to both sides, perusing his surroundings, realizing that he again felt no pain, an experience he did not oppose, realizing how hard he had landed.

The cold, uninviting surroundings of the sewer were intriguing to Thomas. It was nothing more than a hundred-twenty-five-cubic foot box. The man-made rock had no decorations excepting the small trace of moisture that had stained the wall below the opening which led out of the curb on the adjacent street.

He refused to move, not for relaxation, but to heal his body mostly from the sun moments before. He stared up at the entrance he fell from, paying no attention to the two tunnels that led out of the cube near his head and feet. His mind revolted at every inkling of movement. Whether his body wanted to move or not, his brain was reacting as if he were on his deathbed. Every thought was draining energy and he was going to remain motionless until it was no longer a possibility.

As he lay in corpse pose, his senses honed in on the rest of the particulars of his current location. The walls were crawling with miniscule insects, which he assumed to be gnats and fleas. It was a constant moving portrait of a bug metropolis as they weaved around each other in an attempt to scurry to the next driest spot on the wall. Although this image transfixed Thomas's eyes for some time, the potency of the sewer's aroma quietly grew stronger and stronger until Thomas no longer had the ability to ignore it. It was familiar yet uninvited as it conjured up memories of bathroom trauma and rotten fruits found months later in his refrigerator. To his dismay, the longer he lay in the funk, the more it seeped into his other senses, tasting and almost feeling the touch of the sickening scent.

He found himself staring at his hands, trying to bounce the focus of the stench out of his psyche. It was no use. No matter what he focused on, his newly hardened fingernails, oddly sharpened teeth, and even his unusually slick hair could not derail his nose. Still lying on the floor, he resolved his annoyance with the idea that the stench was better than the sunlight, at least he was not in pain.

Turning his attention back to the bugs on the wall, he noticed that he could hear water running from inside the tube he was adjacent to. Birds chirped from up above. Placing his hands flat on the ground at his sides, he scraped his right middle finger across the cold, unforgiving concrete floor of the gutter, sounding as though it were a chalkboard. It gave a tingle to every vertebrae of his spine. Every sound was becoming so intense he convinced himself he was listening to the microscopic bugs' legs pushing off the walls of his makeshift bed.

It was hours before Thomas would move, his mind obsessed with his sudden keen hearing abilities. Listening to the sounds of dust bounce along the floor was washed away as a car drove by, forcing his auditory control to leave the detailed view it was using and return to the macro-audio world he had previously been accustomed to. Had it not been for the rotation of the Earth, Thomas might have spent eternity where he was, but as soon as the sunlight crept onto his shin, he was up and moving.

He spent no time conversing with himself on which way to move. He, instead, took the tunnel nearest his head and crawled into the darkness away from the burn of the sunlight. The short apex of the tunnels forced Thomas to remain on his hands and knees as he sloshed the sewage water through the steel-ribbed tubes. He was being drawn, unaware, to something down in the sewer's depths.

Every time Thomas scooted his body farther into the dark chasm, the sounds of rats scampering through the rotting sewage became more and more prevalent. Every so often he would catch a glimpse of one of the rodents frantically clawing at the iron tube, trying to escape from the path of the odd invader to their world. All the rats and an occasional opossum seemed to be fearful of Thomas and utilized all of their energies trying to scatter.

Thomas continued crawling down the tube as it drove him farther and farther away from his entrance. He looked back to see where he came from and realized that the room was no longer in sight. He was shocked to realize there was absolutely no light visible in the tunnel, yet, his sight remained. In fact, he thought he had better vision in the darkness than he did out in the sun where everything was left an oozing blob of colors.

He kept crawling, mechanical movements, no intelligent thought, dripping in sewage. It was hours of wallowing in filth with no real purpose; he had no destination to end his journey. Not tired, he felt he must keep moving. It did not take long before he realized that he was in an underground grid of the city. Every five minutes or so he came across a small room with either a manhole directly above him or a room similar to the one he fell into with the runoff entrance.

His muscles had not pulled back in fatigue as he continued to crawl though the sewers, utilizing more than half of his day. By this time, he could not escape the funk of the caverns. It had seeped into his skin, allowing the terrible smell to waft straight through him as he journeyed on. With perfect vision, Thomas looked over his shoulder to see nothing but the perfectly clear dark path from whence he had come. It threw him off. He had been expecting all day to find someone following behind. He constantly heard another person on his trail, but the stranger seemed to be invisible or only in his mind.

As he turned back from looking for his nonexistent stalker, Thomas felt an odd pressure on his kneecap. His leg instinctively paused in midair, waiting for an examination before continuing his crawl. Balanced on his left shin, he put his right foot flat on the slimy sewer floor. Pulling his chin into his neck, he looked down at his knee to see a foreign object which had broken the skin and lodged itself into the flesh between his kneecap and the joint.

Horror rushed through his veins as images of amputation due to tetanus filled his brain. He looked closer at the object and noticed it was an old, rusted nail, now dripping with the greenish sludge that flowed slowly throughout the sewage system. His right hand immediately flew up to his leg to swipe the nail from its captor. It took the force of a toddler to remove the rusty splinter. The severity of the injury was quickly apparent as the kneecap moved an inch or so to pop back into its rightful place. The sight of such a disturbing maneuver sent chills through Thomas's body, but it was the fact that he was in no physical discomfort that forced him to reexamine the wound.

Upon closer inspection, he could see the inside of his knee from the large opening left by the nail. There was no blood. The injury looked as if it had been inflicted on an embalmed cadaver. No life force was present, no color, nothing but the mechanics of the human body with a small amount of clear liquid dripping from the wound.

Suddenly, a light splash came from behind Thomas. He swiveled his head around fast enough to cause head trauma, but there was no one there. Confused and slightly unnerved, he turned his attention back to his knee to find the gash had completely healed over. Not even a scar.

His voyage through the sewers was nearly over, as within minutes he came into a new room. Unlike the majority of the rooms he found, this one was not so much a grid point as it was a center point. Coming out of the tubes he had been bent over in all day, he stepped down into a deeper pool of the sewer mire.

Now thigh deep in the disgusting concoction, he could stand entirely erect and survey the area. It was the same concrete material making the room itself, but it was a circular space filled with the same stench, the same bugs, and same rodents he been dealing with his whole adventure. Ten tunnels lined the wall surrounding the center of the room which housed an iron ladder that led up to a manhole. The manhole had a singular hole, allowing the light of the day to shine down upon the ocean of waste in a pinpoint spotlight.

Thomas perused the room, shaking the gunk from his clothes, feeling as though he were not the only person in that room and knowing it wasn't the rats he was sensing. He stood there in a frozen state, trying to avoid the sewage as much as possible while allowing the ideas of his murders to infest his mind. He reflected on the fact that he was now a murderer. A fugitive running from the police for a crime he felt he was justified in committing.

It was starting to hurt his head as he dwelled on those ideas for hours, letting the arguments in his head fight back and forth, trying to accept his murderous reality while still attempting to put a realistic spin on his new unearthly powers. His eyes were focused on the small bit of light coming down from the roof for the duration of the internal argument.

Hours of the day passed by. Still feeling no weariness except mental fatigue, Thomas noticed the light-spot he had been staring at had vanished. Not wanting to emerge in the sunlight to be greeted with the torture he felt that morning, Thomas waited to see if the spot would return. After all, the sun may have taken temporary shelter behind a cloud, but it did not return. All his fears drifted away. He felt an unfamiliar relief that he could now return to the surface and be free to roam.

The cold rungs of the iron ladder refreshed Thomas's skin, allowing it to dance with small reactions to the temperature change. He pulled himself up the ladder, step after step, pushing his body up into the air. Holding onto the ladder with one hand, he reached the other up and pressed against the manhole cover. The heavy iron disc easily moved out of its place as if it were a plastic Frisbee, revealing the beautiful post-twilight city.

As Thomas got to his feet in the middle of the street, he lifted his head straight up reminiscent of a howling wolf, directing his vision toward the moon. Taking a deep breath, he soaked up the energy emanating from the luminescent moon, filling his body with fresh vigor that formerly only accompanied a good night's sleep.

Thomas looked to both sides trying to find an activity to engulf himself in when he suddenly realized… he had not escaped the stench of the sewer. It was now ingrained in him.

Known Vampiric Biology

The ingestion of blood feeds the life source of the creature as it creates energy for their biological structure.

Thomas Year 0 Day 33 AV

Thomas's fingers gripped the bricks with more force than should have been physically possible. He no longer felt any connection to his previous life. His memories of his family, his past habits, and even his former self were losing their fondness as he developed an understanding of his superhuman powers.

Hundreds of feet in the air, he hung onto a skyscraper, watching the citizens of the town scamper about in the middle of the night like an overturned ant mound. Having spent weeks living in the sewers, hiding from the sun in the depths of the city's hell, Thomas enjoyed spending time up in the air, lingering over the city like a god watching his creations. That was a common topic in his mind, God. Over the weeks after his miraculous changes, he had considered what had been happening to him. With no real answers, he could only be thankful. Thankful to God that he still had not been arrested for his murders. He was forced out of his apartment, as it was crawling with police, but he was still grateful, regardless of how surreal his world had become.

He let go of his grip of the grey building, free-falling five or six stories before grasping a ledge, abruptly stopping his descent. Closer to the ground, the people looked more like a blurring glow. As the days had passed, people's features became less and less distinct. Now, weeks since he had slept and days since he ate, all he could see was a glowing pulse within people who walked by. He had no hunger, at least not in the traditional sense. There were a few times where he tried to eat fast food, but it did not seem to give him the rejuvenation he was looking for.

To anyone below, Thomas must have looked like a gargoyle hanging from a window ledge. His skin was now as pale as the building itself; all the fat had melted off his body, leaving a lean, muscular specimen hanging from the structure, scoping out the world below. The layout of the city was ingenious from such a high vantage point. There were many center points throughout the design, with roads and neighborhoods connecting each point together. It resembled explosions instead of a simple grid. The library, the courthouse, the mall, the university… They all had their own dedicated areas. Thomas's mind drifted away into the beauty of his hometown, allowing his body to lose focus. His grip slipped and he fell.

He nearly fell to the ground before he found another ledge to catch onto. His motion stopped immediately. He hung there for a few seconds and then dropped to the floor.

The moon was exceptionally bright that night, as full as it could have been. Thomas stepped out of the shadows of the buildings and joined humanity in the lanes of commerce, which had become an uncommon event for him. He spent much time lingering in darkness out of sight of the normal men who utilized the roads at night, hoping that he would remain unseen and free from persecution for his murders. The moonlight was invigorating, an abundance of get-up-and-go streamed through his body, tempting him to bounce up and down along the sidewalk, leaping over people's heads to express his joy, but that was too much for him. He was not "that kind of" guy.

He spent his time quietly strolling along the street being as casual as possible, thanking God for the blessing of keeping him alive that fateful night. He always pushed down the desire to curse God for making him the way he had become and remembered to be thankful for what he had.

Suddenly, Thomas felt a rushing come through his neck as if all the nonexistent blood in his body was rushing into his head, creating a hot, stuffy feeling. He fell to his knees, afraid he was going to start oozing from the eyes. As he put his hands on his face, trying to push the feeling back in, he lost control. He was just a passenger in his human vessel.

Thoughts coursed into his mind, forcing him to look for the weak people who crowded his personal space. The visions he was seeing through his uncontrolled eyes began to mimic those of the daytime: colors were blurring together, lights were becoming intensely bright and the pedestrians around were nothing but bodies with glowing veins pumping blood through their spiritual machine.

He stood up. People seemed to be getting closer. They left only inches on either side of him and before he knew what happening, he was bumping into bodies. Tunnel vision, the scenery was gone, nothing but people hording near him.

Wanting to close his eyes to avoid the mind trip he was on, he desperately tried to regain control of his muscles, but it was to no avail. His body began to move, quickly, through the crowds, moving faster than he had ever traveled in a car. All he could see were bodies flying past him, like a motorcycle driving through a forest. There was body after body, a near miss. He soared through the sea of humans, and then suddenly, he stopped moving.

The background came into focus as the silhouette of a man stood in front of him, digging in a dumpster. There was no body, just some floating, glowing veins housed inside a manly shadow.

Thomas, still just a spectator in his own body, leapt up above the dumpster where he clenched a balcony ledge several stories above the alley. His feet swayed back and forth over the veins in the dumpster. Road kill on the ground of the alley accentuated the desperation of the supposed man looking for sustenance in the oversized garbage can.

The green steel that housed people's discarded items shifted slightly left and right as a body began to take shape around the veins which had been floating in mid-darkened air. The veins faded and the lights returned to their former magnitude. Thomas felt that perhaps his disorderly nightmare was over.

He tried to move his foot in an attempt to regain control, but nothing happened. Seconds later, Thomas felt a growl growing from his throat and upper chest. The sound was subtle, hidden in the noise of the city, never alerting the dirty old man whose feet kept coming off the ground as he dug deeper into the garbage bin. He seemed to be favoring his right arm, as each time he tried to lift a huge piece of garbage, he would drop it back as he winced and recoiled from the offended arm.

Thomas looked to each side, his eyes searching for witnesses. Then his feet swung beneath him as his hand let go of the balcony. He fell with a sensation like airline turbulence until his feet landed squarely on the man's back. The force of the fall caused the man's ribs to crack on the edge of the dumpster.

Thomas, balancing on the man's body, reached down and grabbed his victim by the chin, yanking to the side, pulling the man's head a hundred eighty degrees, breaking the neck bones and leaving the head facing in the opposite direction.

The man was obviously dead as his body immediately went limp and Thomas, still with no control over his own body, squatted down and bit into the corpse's neck. Feeling more and more energized each passing second, he inhaled the blood of the bum. He was not drinking or eating. He was pulling the blood into his lungs and his body began to feel invincible. The corpse quickly turned a ghastly pale and began to shrivel as Thomas withdrew all hydration from it.

When there was no blood left, Thomas stood up and hopped off the edge of the dumpster and onto the concrete. The wound in the man's neck closed up right before Thomas's eyes, leaving no scar. Thomas looked down to see the blood on his hands and his mind snapped.

Suddenly in control of his body once more, he began backing up, trying to escape from the realization of what had just happened. Thoughts pounded him from every direction. That's my third murder. Now I'm eating people? What kind of monster am I? He took off running down the alley. His new sense of invulnerability caused him to recklessly run through the street without care for what was in the way.

He sprinted down the street, stepping on cars, leaping over bridges, nearly flying. What if I left evidence? I'm going to get caught. I saw the police at my apartment. They know I killed the other two. What kind of sadistic person does this? What kind of sadistic person have I become?

Every time his foot crashed onto the ground, he thought he heard another footstep behind him. He would not look back to see who was following him because he was afraid of who or what could keep up with him. Nothing would stop him. He continued sprinting, looking for refuge… somewhere… anywhere.

He leapt up a three-story building with only one

handhold on the way up. On the top, he stopped to gather his thoughts. Doing his best to avoid the inevitable theories of his capture, he reflected about the last month.

Aware of his sensitivity to light and avoidance of the sun, he considered the obvious. Only a vampire drinks blood, avoids the sun, and has superhuman abilities. Although this thought would have shocked and frightened him months ago, it came as a relief now. Suddenly, he felt that he understood what was happening, realizing he was not insane, but a vampire.

He took a deep breath and looked up to the moon and spoke to his Creator, "Thank you, Lord! You have made me a vampire, a creature of the night. I do not understand why, but I will do my best to honor you."

Thomas lay on the roof of the library watching the stars twinkle in the distance while he reflected on everything that had happened. Just the thought of what he had gone through enraged him to the point of physically shaking. It was the same question time after time. Why me? This is not what I wanted. I just want to live my life as normal.

Unfortunately, he knew this was no longer an option. He had abused his chance at a normal life and wasted every moment of it, never living up to his potential. Without telling himself, he knew that God was giving him another chance at living life. It may not be the chance he desired, but it was God being merciful and allowing him to not leave his life an utter waste.

The only issue he could not resolve was why he was forced to endure the inhalation of blood. Maybe it was karma forcing him to look at his life and consider the people he had harmed. The bum may have just been a symbol of all those who had suffered from the unholy life he had been living.

The experience of witnessing a brutal murder for cannibalism from a first-person perspective was one of the most traumatic experiences he had ever endured. The lack of humanity in the initial attack, the gore of forcing his teeth into the man's neck, the whole ordeal had been animalistic. The lack of control left him not feeling human. He knew that he could not let himself go that long without blood again. As a vampire, he must find a way to feed.

How could he believe that God gave him the gift of a second chance, but still be forced to murder the innocent for such a basic function as consumption? Maybe this was his punishment for not letting the robbers take his life. Maybe this was all just a way for the Father of all men to prove he exists, to show Thomas his purpose in the world. He was confused and angry.

Thomas looked to the sky and shouted, "If you wanted me to know you existed, why didn't you give me a sign? How about now? Give me a sign!" He fell to his knees on the asphalted street, an activity which would have left bruises and scrapes before now. But this night, his deadened vampiric nerves felt nothing. Looking left and right, he hoped to receive guidance, but it was no good. He was left kneeling in the road … waiting.

Just as Thomas was going to scream out that God must not exist, the sun began to peek over the buildings. The morning light took the useless breath out of Thomas's lungs the same way a kick to the chest would. This was not a merciful God helping his child. He felt the sunrise was nothing more than extended punishment.

While Thomas was lying on the street with the first light of the day beating down on him with merciless pain, a beautiful vision appeared in front of him. Glistening in the bright reflections of the sun was the sign he was looking for, although he did not recognize it at the time. It was a small church. No large cathedral towers overshadowed the purpose of the house of worship. It was a monument to faith rather than a monument to man's triumph over nature.

As Thomas felt his energy being sapped from his body, he stared at the small brown brick building in awe. The huge oak door stood open, inviting the masses to enter below the large stained-glass portrait of Jesus of Nazareth. Thomas pulled himself toward the Lord's house, dragging his lower body in a military crawl, desperately trying to reach the sanctuary.

Upon arrival at the steps to the door, Thomas mustered up enough energy to stand and walk into the building. He stumbled a little as he passed the dark brown oak doors and entered the worship hall. The old wooden plank floors creaked as he took each labored step toward the next set of doors below a golden cross on the doorframe. The dingy, off-white walls persecuted Thomas, the unnatural, by securing an abnormal silence in the room as he made his way into God's house.

The second set of doors flung open almost before Thomas touched them, revealing a room that could have been there for hundreds of years. It was the picture of worship from centuries before. The area was filled with pews, two rows, all facing the front of the church, their backs to the entrance where Thomas stood. Some old wooden benches were placed next to brick walls with a single window on each opening up to the outside world. The ceiling stood a good sixty feet up in the air adorning chandeliers lit by candlelight which swung softly in the breeze that blew in from the open doors.

There was no dust on the floorboards, at least not in amounts collected large enough to be seen. The light of the sun did not affect Thomas's vision in the way it had been. He could see clearly as he followed the wooden planks along the floor all the way to the front of the church.

There, at the front, stood a large stone altar, wearing the cloths of the season. A white cloth draped over the stone reached nearly to the ground and an intricately designed green cloth was crookedly arranged on top of the white one.

A frail-looking man stood behind the altar looking into his oversized Bible. The man's few stitches of white hair sat completely still upon his otherwise bald scalp. His wrinkles across the back of his neck and hands suggested that he might be as old as the church in which he worked in.

Just as the altar was, the man was clothed with a white

robe under a green sash with a perfectly matching design. He faced a large stained-glass window of the Pearly Gates. They looked dark and ominous this early in the morning as the window faced due west and caught no morning sunlight.

To one side of the altar was an iron spiral staircase that led down into the floor. On the other side, a white door led to a small interior room that was obviously added on since the church was first built.

The man at the front of the church bowed his head to his Bible and clasped his hands together in prayer. He turned to see Thomas wearily standing in the back next to the last set of pews. The holy man shuffled his feet as he quickly made his way to where Thomas was standing.

Excited to help someone down on their luck, the priest began to speak to Thomas as he passed the first set of pews. "My son, please come in and sit down. This is a place of sanctuary for you, whatever your situation." As he approached Thomas, he noticed how unnaturally pale his skin was and the odd shine of his hair. Even his eyes were almost colorless…

The man of God slowed his pace as the stranger who was standing in his church gave him an unholy feeling. His appearance and his presence seemed to be not of this world, but he kept telling himself "all of God's children are welcome."

"Please, sir, sit down. You look as though you need to rest. I am Father Timeus, the priest of this parish. Whatever your issues, we are here to help you," the priest said as he came within feet of Thomas.

Thomas staggered to the side and flopped down in the last pew. He looked up at Father Timeus and saw fear in his eyes that normally only appeared when confronted with death itself. He worried that the priest knew he was a vampire and might not let him rest, but nonetheless, he spoke. "Thank you, Father. My name is Thomas. I have nowhere to go and I am exhausted."

"Do not worry, my son. We take in anyone who is willing to let Jesus into their hearts. You are welcome here. We have some beds downstairs if you need one." Timeus closed his mouth and peered into Thomas's soulless eyes, silently asking God to make the demonic-looking man leave.

"Thank you. You are kind. I would love to lie down for a while." Thomas tried to stand, but was still weak from the ambush he received from the sun minutes earlier.

Timeus put his hand under Thomas's shoulder and helped him up. They slowly walked across the floor to the staircase in the front of the church, each step causing creaking more suitable for a haunted house than a church. Upon reaching the stairs, Father Timeus knelt down to open the door in the floor, as if they were leaving an attic.

The two men descended the staircase below the old floor of the church into a damp and dark room. The basement of the church looked like a dungeon with moisture creeping in through the concrete walls. The room was garnished with six cots set equidistance apart from each other in two rows. The ceiling had four beams to support the altar above. The only addition to the room was a single lightbulb hanging with a pull string.

The priest did not venture all the way down to the water-stained floor. Instead, he remained on the third to the last step and said, "Stay as long as you need. All of God's children are welcome here." With that, he turned and began making the climb back up the stairs, retreating from the unholy man. There was no welcome in his voice and it was obvious he did not want to spend any amount of time in the cellar of the church.

Thomas sat on the center cot and turned out the light. When the priest reached the top of the stairs, he closed the door, leaving Thomas alone in perfect darkness. He lay down on the cot staring up at the lightbulb, invisible in the blackness, but still swinging back and forth from the momentum Thomas had put into the object when he pulled the string. His eyes did not adjust to the darkness.

He lay totally still. It was the first time since he became a vampire that he did not feel like he was being followed. He still did not feel alone, but it was a comfortable, secure feeling this time.

The coldness started to overtake his body so he turned to his side and curled up into a fetal position. Although the room was much like the sewer system gutters, a concrete box, it had a different feel to it. It was cozy. Or maybe he felt different here since he could not see in the dark anymore. He felt more normal, tired, but normal.

He lay there for a long time; it felt like days, but he

could not sleep. He had not slept since the transition, so it was not a surprise to him. It was more of a disappointment than anything else. But he was feeling better and he knew that his body needed that time to heal itself from the overworked night and the pain the sun caused that morning.

He let his mind wander for hours while he lay on that cot, allowing many theories to birth in his head. Most of the ideas fled his brain as quickly as they arrived, but one that stuck around was the realization that the church was God's way of protecting him. He could have been thrown out. He knew that was what Timeus had wanted to do. He saw it in the priest's eyes, but he was allowed to stay. He was given a chance to apologize to God for his sins. God was merciful after all. Finding the church was not a sign, but a conversation with the Lord himself, spoken through actions rather than words.

Once he came to these conclusions, he felt he had a purpose. God was not punishing him by turning him into a vampire. God's divine plan for Thomas was no more a punishment than Job's tribulations or Jesus' crucifixion. His transition into vampirism was to save Thomas and turn him into a beacon of truth, a messenger of God.

Thomas's attention was constantly diverted by the creaking of the floorboards above. Daily activities of the church required lots of movement inside the old structure of the building. It did not keep him awake, as he was not going to be able to sleep anyway, but his thoughts were not given the attention they deserved. It may have been a good thing; he felt his ideas should remain holy in the house of the Lord and that may not have been the case had he been allowed free reign over them.

The entire day had been spent in blackness within the small room with no adjustment by his eyes. He was left without his security light, the single point of entry in the sewer room where he had stayed. There was no such point of light in the basement and after what felt like an eternity, he decided to rise out of his tomb and return to the surface.

Ascending the staircase brought a familiar experience which had been absent for months. He felt as though he had to use some energy to get up the staircase, not strenuous, but it was more noticeable than running down the street or leaping onto balconies had been. Each step left a clanging sound echoing in the room below as his tattered and mildewing sneakers found traction on each stair. Reaching the top step, he lifted his hand above his head to push open the door to reveal the historic splendor of the church.

Emerging from his hole, Thomas felt like he was walking into a new world where tradition was beauty and faith ruled over logic. As he looked at the chandeliers hanging still from the lofty ceiling, he noticed the candles were not lit, yet it was light inside the building.

He looked to one of the side windows. It was still daylight outside. He turned to go back down into his pit when the light shining in the stained-glass mural of the Pearly Gates caught his eye. It was a glorious picture of ornate golden gates partially open to allow men to enter the splendor of heaven. In the center of the stained glass was a small circle of uncolored glass, leaving a tiny vision to the outside world. He took a deep breath and noticed he could feel his pulse for the first time since he became a creature of the night.

He bowed his head slightly and thanked God for giving him this chance, this second try at life. Pulling his head up from his brief prayer, he looked to his side to find Father Timeus speaking with a short woman. They stood at the back of the church just as he did when he first arrived. He could not hear their conversation nor could he sense their moods. After weeks of peering into people's lives with no effort or permission, he felt as though he were missing an innate ability. He compared his lack of intensified senses to someone losing the ability to walk. He had been taking it for granted and felt crippled without it.

He moved away from the stairs and slowly crept toward the pair. He wanted to be anonymous and stealthy, but every movement his body intended to make caused the floor of the church to scream in its symbolic squeaks from the age of the old wood. The smallest movements threatened to blow Thomas's cover as he tried desperately not to be noticed. His stare was intense and unwavering. He could not pull his gaze away. Something about the situation drew him to it.

The white cassock of the priest contrasted with the dark black hair of the woman he was talking to. She stood with a rounded back, a posture that gave her the image of being completely submissive. She mostly looked down at the floor. The occasional glance up at the priest allowed Thomas to see her features. She was still young, most likely in her late twenties, but there was obvious experience on her face. She bore the marks of a woman who has felt her fair share of pain from life.

The priest was emphasizing his conversation with hand gestures and constantly waved his hand over her head. Although he was a short man, he stood well over a foot taller than she. Had she lifted her head and squared her back, they may have rivaled each other's height.

Thomas felt a strange connection to the woman. It was not a romantic love at first sight, at least not one that he recognized. The sensation was one of pride and love, something rarely felt outside of the relationship between a parent and their children. With no experience to draw from, he could not understand the feeling. He believed her to be beautiful, seeing past her scars and the time-worn effects to the true identity within. She either had an addiction she was battling or was starving to death, told clearly by the bones that left a clear outline through her skin over each part of her body.

She looked up past the priest and looked directly into Thomas's eyes, causing him to abashedly look away, avoiding her recognition of his gawking. As he looked up to the ceiling, he caught a short glimpse of her face. Her cheekbones seemed to protrude from her skull with sunken-in eyes that had no faith in humanity or nature. Her dull black hair swung forward with the thrust of her head, causing the long strands to sway around arms and hips at the tips of their extension.

In a panic, Thomas refused to look away from the ceiling, afraid that she was still looking at him, disapproving of his ogle. He watched the crystal in the chandeliers glisten with different reflections as the light of the outdoors began to wane and the sun retreated to the east. It was the movement of his shirt as the woman walked by him that alerted his senses to the fact that it was OK for him to look down again. He turned back to look at the woman and watched her descend the stairs into the basement, exiting from his view.

With no hope of looking uninterested, Thomas turned and began a brisk pace, attempting to reach the priest as quickly as possible. Father Timeus had begun straightening the Bibles in the cubby on the back of a pew when Thomas spoke to him in a slightly rushed manner. "Who, uhhhh, who were you talking to?" He worried that it might not be any of his business.

Timeus looked up at Thomas, assuming that the young man was experiencing puppy love due to his poorly masked interest in the young lady. "Lilith is just another of God's children seeking guidance." He decided to leave it at that. No need to encourage lust. Then he began the subject that he felt was important for Thomas's spirituality. "You were very tired this morning and I didn't get a chance to really speak with you. What brought you to our doorstep?" The priest had to force his fears of the young man aside.

Thomas wanted to avoid people knowing about his vampirism, so he spoke in code. "I was down on my luck and I just sort of stumbled in here." He needed to make sure the priest did not press the issue, so he redirected the conversation. "Why did you join the ministry?"

The abrupt change in subject seemed to miff the priest a bit, so Thomas continued in an attempt to transition to his new topic. "I spoke to God yesterday. I think I have a calling, not to run a church or preach or anything like that, but I think God has a very specific job for me. Did you always know or was your calling an unexpected change in your drive?"

Father Timeus was taken aback by Thomas's interest in his calling from God, but was excited to share his experience with him. "It was a shock when I felt the Lord guide me to my purpose in this world. I was studying to be a lawyer at the time, finishing up my prelaw degree and preparing to take the LSAT.

"One day I was spending an afternoon at a coffeehouse just off the edge of campus studying for my test when I saw a squirrel run across the street. The little animal scurried around the cars that were driving down the lanes when it froze in the middle of the road. Just when it looked like it was going to be run over by a truck, it jumped onto a telephone pole, narrowly escaping death."

The priest walked past Thomas over to a pulley system. He continued his story as he turned the crank, allowing the chandeliers to descend to the ground. "It hit me that the squirrel could have been killed right there, just like any of us at almost any moment. I knew that I wanted to be lawyer because I wanted to help people, but it was only a type of monetary assistance. I would be helping people get some money for when they were wronged, but that wouldn't help people in the long run. So I reflected for a long time on what to do." Father Timeus finished turning the crank and slowly walked over to the grounded chandeliers to light the candles.

"One day I went to church, which was a seldom occurrence for me and God spoke to me through the priest. He talked about moving your life in a new direction and taking a leap of faith to do what you know in your heart you need to do, even if it leaves you uncomfortable."

Father Timeus droned on about how God was righteous and he needed to enlighten the world, but Thomas had drifted off into his own thoughts. The reflexive movements of the priest lighting the candles acted as focal point while Thomas fell into his hypnotic state, considering how lost he had been in his life before gutting religion from his routine after he was forced to attend mass as a small child. God must have been correcting the situation now by drawing him to a church for shelter. Or maybe he was chosen and he had a greater purpose, just like he told the priest. Maybe there was more truth to his words than he thought.

Father Timeus was still telling his story. "Knowing that I needed to spread the Word of God, I took great solace in the divine plan, because God has a plan for everybody, no matter how important or unimportant things may seem."

Thomas awoke from his trance to hear the last few words the priest had told him and he had to interject, "So, it is all in God's plan?" Thomas was having an awakening as his mouth continued to move. "I was saved during a robbery. Not saved like I was born-again, but truly pushed out of death's grip. God saved my life, and he did it for a reason. Those thieves should have killed me, but I was salvaged. God was speaking to me, saving me from thieves, allowing me to save others from the same fate. He gave me a mandate to rid the world of robbery. 'Thou shall not steal!'" Thomas's voice was amplifying as he put these ideas together in his head.

Father Timeus lit the final candle and started to make his way back to the lever on the wall. He knew that Thomas was getting amped up, but what he was saying was sounding dangerously like a vigilante. "I am glad you are having a dialogue with God and I can't know what your role in his plan is, but that doesn't sound like the job of man. We all have free will and I can't believe that God would want you to take away that choice from his children." The priest was hoping this would strike a chord with Thomas.

Thomas, now teeming with energy, started to make his way toward the doors, ready to go out into the night. The stained-glass gates had returned to their dark and foreboding appearance as the only light shining through them was the glimmer of the newly risen moon. But he wanted to finish his conversation before he left.

"You spread the Word of God; you are his voice. I understand now that I am to enforce the Word of God. I am his hand, his angel. He wants to work through me."

Thomas turned to leave the church, but as a priest, Father Timeus felt he must try to stop him from committing more sins. "God will allow you this decision, but before you go and sin in his name, is there anything you would like to confess? Maybe I can help clear up your confusion about your purpose on this earth."

Thomas stopped inches from the threshold of the door. With great speed, he turned back to face the priest. His eyes bore holes in the priest's psyche. His annunciation increased, leaving his sharp vampire teeth as Father Timeus's primary focus. "I spoke to God this morning. He led me to this church to make sure I knew that I was to honor his name. I don't need you to mediate between my Lord and myself. There is no confusion on what I am to do." In his head Thomas added, He made me a vampire; he made it so I have to sin to exist.

Thomas turned back forcing the doors open with an extreme force as the priest watched him walk out into the entryway and out the oak doors. Timeus's heart was pounding in his chest, driven by fear and nearing failure. Standing with his hand on the crank for the chandeliers, the priest bowed his head, trying to slow his pulse. He was afraid he did not try hard enough when he heard something in the back of his head, which he identified as God, say, "The devil sends men who believe they are right." At that point, he decided Thomas was not an angel, but possibly a minion of Satan.

Letter to the Pope

There may be a demon in my congregation.

Timeus Year 76 Day 194 AB

The priest sat in his office looking deeply into the crosses that adorned his walls. He had never before dealt with a force such as Thomas. Just the look of the pale young man brought fear to Father Timeus's soul. The world did not seem to make sense anymore.

He bowed his head, looking for answers. Speaking to God in the most intimate way, he questioned the purpose of the demonic-drenched boy. He received no answers, which did not come as a surprise to the priest as he concluded, long ago, that the phrase "speaking with God" was not to be literally translated.

He scratched his old, cracking fingernails across the new plastic of his desk. Money in the church was spent on meaningful items and his desk was not one of them. The small plastic and metal structure swayed with nearly every breath Timeus took. Nothing brought peace to his mind.

Questions flowed through his head. Am I being tested? Is it God or Satan tempting me to drop my faith with the evil that treads through this holy building so nonchalantly? Why can't I hear your word when that monster claims to have spoken to you?

His questioning directed toward God was not a new issue for the priest. Ever since his time in seminary, he envied other men who claimed to speak to the Lord, an activity he typically came to deny. There was no way someone as faithful as he had been, someone who tore his life asunder to preach the Word of God, could not be allowed to hear the voice of the divine.

Father Timeus took a deep breath, letting his cynical side turn toward his own faults as opposed to the perceived ones of God. The skepticism hit hard when he began to relive his most despicable of actions.

He lay his face on the cool, wobbly surface of the plastic, picturing his youth in his head. The boy who haunted his teenage mind became so clear again. His light red hair curled atop his head, shadowing over the ever gleeful face that he possessed. It was a painful sight, one that he never wanted to see again.

He was only twelve years old at the time. The late nineteen forties housed the memory perfectly as he remembered the war ending and everyone around town being so happy. It was the worst situation for your best friend to kill himself. He almost felt guilty to be unhappy, as if he were unpatriotic, but he was betraying his childhood if he did not grieve for his childhood chum.

Had it not been Timeus's fault he may have been able

to get past it. But his reaction to the sexual come-on of his schoolmate sent him screaming. He threatened to tell the boy's parents, called him names, even threw a few punches as the last thing he wanted to do was kiss a boy.

That was enough to drive a young gay child to suicide. A funeral that was surrounded by the pride of a tyrant brought down. Maybe that was the issue for the priest. He mourned for his dead friend, but because he missed the companionship, he was not repentant. He was somewhat glad the boy would not come on to him again. He almost felt some tyranny ended in his own small world.

Still sitting at his desk, the priest wondered if he were evil himself. Years of acting out to mask his hatred of himself culminated in his entry into the seminary.

He laughed to himself as he thought about the squirrel story he always told to explain his entrance into the church, but it was false. He was there to keep himself from being a murderer, a thief, or any number of other things he was on track to become. The church was his refuge.

He stood up to go check on Lilith, still letting the ideas roll through his head about how to get rid of Thomas. He just wanted to move on with his life, with Thomas gone forever.

Known Vampiric Biology

An uncontrollable desire for blood can take over the body when the vampire has not fed in some time.

Thomas Year 0 Day 114 AV

Adrenaline flowed through Thomas's body. He was thrilled to know his purpose as he ran down the sidewalk in joy. The night he spoke to Father Timeus was not the first night he began killing in the name of God. He realized that God would tell him when the time had come. If he was not losing control then, there was no need to do anything because God was not telling him to. He spent weeks analyzing what he was doing and why he was doing it. In the end, he decided that he had to feed. It was a part of survival, but in honor of God's rescue of his soul, he would only feed on thieves and robbers. He would help rid the world of their sins.

Night after night, he would stalk suspicious-looking people, following them from above, witnessing their actions and judging them for their sins. He would observe crimes that he told God he could stop, but without the physical permission from his savior, he was just a stalker, waiting for his time to ascend. Lists of criminals were tracked in

Thomas's head, knowing that one day he would get the urge and know that God had given him the permission he was looking for.

After months of waiting and convincing Father Timeus that he is going to be an upstanding citizen, it happened. The sun had just recently set, leaving the sky a beautiful dull orange that was fading quickly. Thomas pushed open the large oak doors of the church and stepped out into the world. Leaving the Lord's house, he felt his vampiric biology take over, watching people's veins become visible while the details that identified them vanished. His hearing began to catch every little sound, and everyone's emotions were on display for him only.

But this day was a little different. People's blood pumping through their bodies glowed with such passion that it began to mask the background. He could hear pulse rates as people walked by, sounding like a steady stream of waves crashing around him. He knew that if he did not eat this night, he might lose control again.

He ran the list through his head, trying to pinpoint someone to target. His conscience tapped him on the shoulder, trying to force him to appreciate the horrible deed he was planning on doing, but he had told himself a thousand times, "I have to save the innocent by eliminating the sinners." He had made the judgment and was OK with taking a life as long as it was a life he felt was not worth being lived. It was not different than the two robbers who were going to kill him. He was saving lives by erasing the wicked. He had to act quickly before the devil would take over his actions and take any life that was in the way.

He leapt up to the top of a building by bouncing back and forth between two walls close enough that he could easily make the jumps. Upon reaching the top of the three-story stucco pawnshop, he decided upon whom he would prey. Without slowing his pace, he leapt from the building, bouncing off a streetlight to get to the next set of roofs.

Heading toward the train station near the bad side of town, he felt like a superhero, flying through the night sky by springing from one building to another, going from light pole to balcony like no normal human had ever done. He passed his old apartment as well as the strip club he once frequented, no tempting thoughts of naked women even flirted with his mind now. He was a changed being, an angel, holy and pure.

His destination was the home of a man whom he had seen break into a pawnshop and mug two people. Watching people commit crimes in which Thomas felt was his duty to stop was a punishing activity. He forced himself to watch sin being carried out and not act on it in order to be assured that he could feed in the future.

The man who was the vampire's target lived in a low-end area of town inhabited by many criminals: drug dealers, murderers, gang members, prostitutes, and it was not too far from where Thomas last paid rent. Unfortunately for that man, being a thief was what would end his life.

It was an old neighborhood where the man was found by Thomas. Derelict cars lined the streets and occasionally found their ways into the homeowners' yards. The road itself was cracked and uneven, desperately in need of repair by the city, but as was the case with most tax-paid services, if you were not the upper crust, then you would not receive the assistance you desired. There were no garages and a thousand square foot floor plan would have dwarfed the majority of the houses. But it was an old wooden house with yellow paint chipping and falling off where Thomas ended up standing, peering into a window at his prey.

The man was short and fat, not slightly overweight, fat. Still somewhat early in the evening, the man sat on his couch staring into the television, allowing the chili he was eating to slowly drip down his chins and onto his faded Hawaiian print shirt. If there were ever a picture of gluttony, this was it.

The flashing of the television lighted the otherwise darkened room in random colors and created flashes of glittery images across the man's blond stubble that reached all the way down from his jaw through the folds down to his chest. Disgusted, Thomas could do nothing other than wait for the man to commit another sin of stealing.

Nearly an hour passed before the man finally turned the television off with his remote and swayed from side to side in what was probably a daily struggle to get off his couch. He lifted both feet high in the air then slammed them to his ruined hardwood floors, trying to create enough momentum to get his obese body to his feet. His posture caused more issues with his ability to stand than anything else with his butt and lower back flat against the seat of the couch and only his shoulders touching the backrest.

Eventually, the man defeated gravity and made it to his full stature. He grabbed a knife and a ski mask in preparation for his nightly work. Then he waddled out the door and straight into the street to man his twenty-year-old hatchback.

Thomas's amazing speed left no challenge for him to keep up with the fat man sputtering down the road in his two-decade-old car. Thomas jumped from building to light pole to telephone pole, all the while keeping one eye on the old beat-up black, three-door economy car. A right turn, a left turn, an occasional U-turn did not slow down Thomas in the least, running after the car on the telephone wires as if he were on a tightrope.

Known Vampiric Biology

The life source appears to be a type of venom capable of healing wounds.

Thomas Year 0 Day 115 AV

Eventually the one-sided chase ended in a neighborhood quite the opposite from where the fat man lived. Million-dollar homes constructed on oversized lots, each being the castle of its territory. Fiats and Lamborghinis lined the driveways, with many sitting in the halo of perimeter security lighting.

It was there that the fat man parked his car and ventured farther into the neighborhood on foot, peering into the front door of each house that had its lights out and no cars in front. He spent hours looking into doors, trying to find the perfect target, the house with no one home and no security system. The house he would eventually select did have a security system, but he could see the control pad from the front door and it was not armed.

Thomas darted from bush to porch, avoiding any light, being as stealthy as possible as he stalked his prey. His vision intensified as he waited for the man to settle on a target. He feared he might lose control before he would get the opportunity to attack. After much time, the fat man moved his car to the driveway of the unsecured home in preparation for his entry and escape.

With his car in plain view, the obese robber wobbled around the side of the mansion to find a window large enough for him to squeeze through. Thomas hid behind a juniper across the street. The small prickles did not affect his deadened nerves. Peering between the small green vegetation, he witnessed the short, fat man pull out a crowbar and somehow forced it under the window ledge, popping the window open with a sound that should not have been audible to Thomas. The man's pudgy arms pushed the window up above his head and threw his waist up onto the ledge. However, his equilibrium shifted, his feet flew up in the air, and he inadvertently dove into the house headfirst.

Thomas, although still in control, had entered into a different mode. He was now a hunter. As soon as the fat man was in the house and out of sight, Thomas was out from behind the plant. He accelerated quickly, taking huge steps to get to the intruder. Two steps got him across the oversized lawn as he leaped over the street to the other yard. He eyed the window to make sure his food was not trying to escape.

Instantly, he came to an immediate stop directly in front of the window. His eyes instantaneously adjusted to the darkness of the house's interior, seeing the fat man with perfect vision. The glow of the burglar's veins felt as though they were burning Thomas's retinas. Thomas prepared to enter through the window as the man walked with both arms straight out, stiff, using them as his eyes, resembling a zombie wandering the earth. The blubber crammed through a doorframe and he exited the initial room.

Thomas gracefully jumped in through the window and landed in a kneeling position inside the house with one hand flat on the ground and the other swiping his hair out of his eyes.

His vampiric instincts told him to keep moving once he was in the house, but he could not shake the feeling he was being followed. He looked around, out the window, but saw no one. No movement, no blowing curtains from someone running away, no faint scent of someone hiding, nothing. He refocused his attention and darted through the house.

He could hear every particle of dust that was moving in the mansion and his target was just a few rooms over. Within seconds, Thomas sprinted through the hallway. He narrowly missed some drywall and quickly entered into the master bedroom where the fat man was.

Thomas stood in the doorway looking at the man's grotesque back as he dug into the enormous dresser. The man tossed underwear on the floor as he dripped sweat all over the place while frantically looking for something of value. The cherry wood chest of drawers was the centerpiece of the room. The California king-sized pillow-topped bed stood back and to the side. Ornate lamps were on the edge of the room, but the dresser with the fifteen-foot mirror atop it was directly in front when you entered the room.

The fat man looked over his shoulder to see if anyone had come home and caught him, but he did not see Thomas, who was hovering over the man's other shoulder. Standing over him and watching the sinful man filled Thomas with the righteous anger of the Lord, leaving him wanting to exact revenge, but something told him to calm down. He was not there to punish men. It was not his place. Instead, he was there to cleanse the world of sin. Instead of seeking revenge and letting the man know he was about to meet his Maker, he simply grabbed onto the man's skull and before the sensation even triggered the fat man's brain, his neck was broken.

Thomas stood there holding onto the fat man's skull, his massive body dangling from the suspended head. Silently, he bent over to feed. He instinctively opened his mouth to the point where his jaw nearly unhinged and plunged his fanged row of teeth into the corpse's back.

This time in full control of his actions, he felt the pure joy in draining the blood from the corpse. Thomas began to feel a tingle in his lips and the sensation travelled through to every corner of his body. The warm liquid dripped down his throat, coating his esophagus and lungs, causing him to shiver with pleasure. The last bit of blood left the body and was absorbed into Thomas's tongue. Finished, he let the body fall to the ground where the wounds would soon heal over.

As Thomas turned to return to the church feeling useful to his God, he caught a glimpse of a man running down the hall back toward the room Thomas had entered from. Using his supernatural speed, he launched himself down the hall in pursuit of his witness. He heard nothing, sensed nothing, and by the time he got out the window, he saw nothing. Realizing how in tune his senses had been, he knew there could not have been anyone there. Feeling satisfied and righteous, he returned to the church, the place he now thought of as home.

Jack's Diary

I confronted him today. I hoped I would feel for him as my child, but he is just an annoyance.

Thomas Year 1 Day 7 AV

A year had passed since Thomas began his mission to serve God through the extermination of thieves. Everything remained the same during that time: Thomas fed every couple of months, Father Timeus feared the demonic forces behind Thomas's words, and Lilith remained an intriguing mystery. The light of the moon was the only natural light Thomas ever saw anymore. He liked to reminisce about the old days, when he could walk the town during the day, interact with people without invoking odd emotions, and eat real food to relieve his hunger.

He was not upset about his current situation. He had learned to enjoy time to himself while having free roam over the entire city from top to bottom at night. He had learned to sneak into buildings just as they closed, leaving him the ability to spend time reading in the library or watching movies in theatres. He truly felt the city was his personal playground.

But he did miss a few things that never returned after

his transformation. He no longer felt lust or sexual desire in any way. He was able to seduce women with his piercing gaze and insight into their emotions, but he never felt the rush of anticipation unless he was to feed. He did not feel the anguish of loss. And he no longer felt pain as long as he stayed out of the sunlight. It was something he would not have expected to grieve for, but it left him feeling dead. Without physical pain, he constantly questioned his humanity.

As these thoughts rolled through his head for the thousandth time, he hung from a fire escape. His feet were entangled in the rusted ladder while his head hung down, dangling over the robber he was about to kill. He enjoyed hanging from his feet, although he felt it was absurdly cliché for a vampire. But still, the freedom to swing about, pretending to be weightless, was a blast. He watched as the robber tucked his mugging fortunes into his pockets while searching around him looking for the police. It was too bad for him he did not look up, although he could not have escaped Thomas.

Thomas tucked his knees then took a huge jump straight down at the man's head. The speed Thomas achieved in the twenty-foot drop to the man created such force that the robber's chest was crushed and he died instantly upon impact with Thomas's body. Lying on top of the lifeless body, the vampire bit into the neck of the corpse. The typical rejuvenation streamed throughout his veins as he drained the succulent blood from the warm body.

The full moon that night gave Thomas an extra surge

of energy. He tried to stave off feeding until the full moon, but he was not always successful. He let the carcass fall to the ground once he was done drinking, standing up tall, drawing in the lunar power that fulfilled his mind. The dreary mood of the city vanished when he could see the full moon. Constant dirt swirling through the air, the screams of random people, normal for any major city, just dissipated into the background.

He could have stayed there all night, but he had to ditch the body and get back to the church before sunup, so he took in one last glorious look at the moon and turned to grab the deceased. He felt as though someone were watching him, but he had grown accustomed to that feeling as it never seemed to go away except when he was inside the church.

Without taking time to look over his shoulder, he grabbed the dead mugger under its limp arms and carried it like a sack of potatoes in both hands. The wounds in the neck had healed as usual. Thomas clenched the body as he leapt up onto the fire escape two stories up.

His hands were unavailable due to carrying the dead body, so he jumped from a fire escape to a balcony to the roof using only his legs for balance. Once on the roof, he gained speed to leap across the street to the next building on the way to the dumpster he always dropped his leftovers in.

Sixty miles an hour jumping from rooftop to rooftop allowed his vision to move into a type of tunnel vision with a blur of colors around his focus. All of the visual details around him disappeared into the blur. Normally, all sounds blurred into a whoosh, but that night, Thomas heard footsteps pounding from behind him. Without losing any speed, he soared across a chasm in the buildings, looking back in midair and saw a man sprinting behind him.

The man was very tall and slender with peculiarly pale skin. He had a determination drawn across his face that almost startled Thomas as much as the fact that he was keeping up with him. Every step Thomas took he could hear a thunderous pounding of the other man's steps behind him. Thomas tried to move faster, but the steps kept outpacing his. Before he knew it, the man passed him, jumping over his head and landing right in Thomas's path.

He tried to stop, but he could not. The two men and the corpse fell to the roof they were racing across. Thomas came to a quick realization that he had indeed been followed for the last year. Filled with rage to the point of shaking, he screamed at the cadaverous-looking man, "Who the hell are you, and why have you been following me?"

The man looked at Thomas. His eyeballs had no color other than the pitch-black of the pupil. He cocked his head to his left just a tiny bit, and then cracked a smile, showing his long, sharp teeth. The man was obviously a vampire from his razor-sharp grille. Seeing the sharpened set gleaming in his direction gave him a new understanding of the fear people portrayed when they came into contact with his smile.

The man looked to be in his late teens. His tight skin, although nearly translucent, gave the impression of very little wear and tear on his body. He had long, silky, dark bluish locks with eyes that seemed to pop out of his head. The triangular shape of his head, like that of an upside down pyramid, made him appear very sinister.

The mysterious vampire opened his mouth like he was going to answer Thomas, but instead, let out a high-pitched shrieking laugh that would have hurt a normal man's eardrums. With that, he grabbed the corpse by the wrists and jumped off the edge of the building. Thomas was in shock. He had no idea what was going on. In an instinctive move to get some answers, he jumped over the edge of the building as well.

Falling headfirst down the side of the fifty-story building was no longer a rush for Thomas. He felt more anticipation from the chance encounter with another vampire than the fall. Seconds into the drop, the unknown vampire landed on his feet and looked up to see Thomas hurtling toward him. He took a couple of slow steps to the side, and then bolted down the street. Thomas turned his body so he was upright as his feet hit the concrete, then he pushed with his legs to give chase to the stranger.

Tearing down the road, Thomas watched the vampire leap to tremendous heights, much higher than he was able to pull off. One step the vampire would bounce over the streetlights, then next, he was over four-story buildings. Every now and then he would reach ten stories in the air, nearly disappearing from sight. They continued on their breakneck chase for quite some time.

The two night creatures ended up outside the city and

off the pathways of any roads. Running through brush and bushes, Thomas had difficulty keeping up, even jumping over most of the plant life that stood in his way. The ground was soft and did not give him the proper grip he needed to keep his balance.

Thomas could see in the distance that the other vampire had stopped. He jumped over the last few trees to reach the other vampire, who, by now, was standing in front of a lake with the corpse raised over his head as if he were sacrificing it to the gods. It was an amazing sight. It looked like it belonged on a nature sounds CD cover.

The glistening of the water in the light of the moon created a mystical silhouette with the vampire's thin yet muscular body flexing on every spot of his arm. The baggy-collared shirt wafted in the breeze in sync with the ripples in the water.

Thomas took a few steps toward the man still holding his pose. As he moved a few feet closer, the other vampire took a quick peek over his shoulder to see Thomas inching nearer. He jumped at least fifty feet in the air and flung the dead body from its wrists. The body twirled like a perfectly thrown football with its arms extended due to the centrifugal force. The vampire twisted in the air before his descent began to end up landing back on the ground facing Thomas in perfect synchronization with the body's splash into the lake, disappearing forever into the black waters of night.

Noticing the vampire was facing him with a quizzical stare like that of a bird, Thomas felt this was his chance to try and get some kind of answer. "I figured it out a while ago. We are vampires, right?"

Again, the man grinned, letting the moonlight glimmer off his monsterlike teeth. His eyes bulged from his head and as he leaped over Thomas, he let out a spine-chilling laugh, the unholy of sounds. Off he went again, but Thomas was not going to let him go. He had spent a year wandering the lonely town by himself without the slightest hint of another of his kind.

Back through the thicket, down the road, and back into the city they went, up a building, a tight left turn hanging onto an antenna, the man's legs swinging straight out to the side over the edge of the building with a view down the sixty-story skyscraper. Thomas stayed in perfect pursuit. They jumped across the skyline, tempting fate as the moon had already gone down over the horizon and the sun could appear very soon. They seemed to be making circles and the vampire was constantly climbing higher and looking about. Thomas knew he was looking for something, but what? Was he trying to lose him?

The man seemed to find what he was looking for because he dove off the building he was on, down to a balcony four hundred feet below. Thomas nearly broke the balcony with the force of his pursuing fall. Still following the vampire, he plunged off the balcony to the street below.

Once he landed, he realized they were standing directly in front of the church where he had been sleeping. He turned to talk to the vampire, but the vampire kicked off the manhole cover and slithered onto his hands and knees, crawling backward into the sewer.

Thomas jumped down after him, entering the room where he had spent a month living. The knee-deep sludge remained in the center of the area with the tunnels leading out of the room in every direction. The familiar setting put Thomas at ease, but he was confused about why the vampire wanted to stop there. It was not the most comfortable area in the city and the smell seemed to have grown worse since he had been there.

The man was hanging upside down from his feet on the iron ladder. He looked down at Thomas, still wallowing in the muck of the sewer and finally spoke. "You said you had some questions?"

Thomas squinted his eyes, letting his frustration show on his face, but he was still grateful for the opportunity to find answers to the questions that had been rolling around his head for over a year. "We are vampires, right?"

The man chuckled a bit as he moved his lips to the side trying to pick the perfect answer to the question. "Yes, we are what they call vampires. A vampire may not be what you think, but yes, we are vampires."

Thomas was so excited to finally have someone to confirm his suspicion he could not figure out what to say next. "Then how did that happen? I mean, what is a vampire? Well, I guess I know what a vampire is…"

The other vampire realized that Thomas was overzealous and was not going to be able to form logical questions, so he broke into speech. "My name is Jack. I have been like this for an atrocious amount of time. There is much to learn, but it must be divulged slowly as it is too much of a shock to hear it all now. Just so you are aware, I am responsible for your rebirth. It was an accident. I hope you will forgive me, but I hope that we can make the best of this. I have been watching you from afar, and you have been very responsible with your feedings. You have not multiplied and created another in your feedings."

Thomas was getting antsy with Jack's slow delivery of the information that he had been dying to hear. He had to interject because the smell of the sewer was getting to him. "Can we go back up to the street?"

Jack's eyes opened wider than looked possible. The question caught him off guard. "This is the safest place to speak in the region. You never know who is listening to your conversations." Then he reached his hands past his head and grasped a ladder rung. Releasing his feet, he flipped over and landed upright in the sewage.

"I know you want to ask questions and learn about your existence, but it is crucial you understand what is happening inside you." Jack droned on about how they needed blood for their biology to exist and draining it from others was the only possibility. He warned Thomas of not draining all the fluids from his victims as the vampiric venom that flowed through their bodies kept them alive and healthy and they would mingle with a victim's blood. If the victims were not completely dead beforehand, they would rise as a vampire.

Thomas, forgetting where he was, fell back in shock onto his butt, splashing the sewage up into his face. There was no avoiding the smell now that he was submerged in the stench. Having heard the entire warning, the only thing that stuck in his mind had to be asked. "So, you turned me into a vampire?"

Jack joined Thomas sitting in the muck of the sewer and elaborated on what had happened. "I only feed on the dead because it is safer that way. Then there is no chance of changing a man. I heard gunshots from the building you were in so I went to relieve my hunger. All three people looked to be dead. No one was moving or breathing, so I started with you. When I bit you in the convenience store and you sat up, it shot terror through my heart. I knew when my mouth came off of your skin you would make the change. It is a fate I vowed years ago to never impose on another man and I am sorry."

Thomas was becoming more and more convinced that it was divine intervention. After the robbery, he could not force himself to move. He was bit by a vampire who preys only on the dead, and having chose him out of three choices, it must have been God's will. "So, there are more of us?"

Jack nodded his head slowly as he played in the greenish water, letting it pool in his hands. "Yes, there are vampires all over the world, but we are an independent group. We rarely congregate and try to avoid each other. There tends to be a lot of conflict when we get together."

"Then why are you here with me?"

"You were my mistake and I must take responsibility for your actions until you go off on your own."

Thomas was concerned about being "a mistake," even though he believed he had a larger purpose. It was disconcerting hearing someone label him as such. He felt that maybe he would gain a larger understanding if he understood Jack more. Maybe he could get a real insight into why he did not want to be around vampires and why he was so upset to have turned Thomas. "How did you become a vampire?" Thomas spoke these words with a smooth, almost sneaky tone.

Jack smirked at the thought, as he had not mused over his rebirth in quite some time. "All right, I guess that is a fair question."

Jack's Diary

Another typical day; the horses are fed and the stable is swept.

Jack Year 0 Day 0

"A small town thrived on the edge of a hill. Peasants diligently toiled away at their daily duties in an effort to keep the kingdom's economy stable. At the top of the hill sat a beautiful castle made of stone and mortar. It was a massive structure with ten wings leading out from the central hall. The king stayed in his fortress overlooking his realm: the small cottages housing his people, the markets where they spent most of their days, the training grounds where his knights became men. Only those who worked in the castle ever saw him, but it was his kingdom.

"Down in the village near the perimeter wall stood a small house of wood and stone. It was a simple cottage housing simple people with simple lives. My mother, Mary, served the king, mostly as a cook, but she was there for any desire he had. She always spoke of him as a good man and claimed to never have been put in a situation she was uncomfortable. My father, Simon, was a baker, running the bakery on the east side of the village. He had no qualm with his place in society; he understood the system and how it worked. I was working as a horse trainer, seventeen years old and already a five-year veteran. I supplied the equines for the knights of the empire.

"Together, we had a reasonable existence for the time period. I had never left the town to venture outside of the walls, which was an adventure reserved only for the warriors who would act on the king's will, slaying dragons and enemies with their brutal might. But on one fateful day, I arose early in the morning before my steeds had awoken for the morning feedings. Wandering outside of my family's house, I took a stroll along the perimeter wall.

"It was that morning in the darkness before the sun welcomed the world over the horizon when I saw him. He was a muscular man with broad shoulders and long legs. He had no hair on top of his head. I first saw him perched atop the perimeter wall an astounding hundred feet in the air. I, worried for the security of the king, shouted at the man, 'Identify yourself! You are not of familiar face.'

"The bulky man looked down from the ledge appearing shocked someone had seen him. He stepped off the edge of the wall and fell to the ground, landing mere feet in front of me. Upon striking the earth, he stood up, standing two feet taller than I stand now. I was taken aback by the death-defying fall, but I did not want to show any weakness by gasping.

"The man spoke to me through my mind. His mouth never moved, and no sound was created. 'I am from a land faraway. You are here to end your miserable life with the most glorious of existences.'

"Up close, I could see the man was dressed in just a loincloth. He had strange symbols burned into his body, lines with the same strange curve in random places across his flesh. I looked up, trying to figure out if I should call for help for this man could be here to spy on the kingdom. 'You have been branded from heel to skull. Are you a leper?'

"Again, words poured into my mind rather than my ears. 'No. I am a wanderer. I am immortal. These are my markings; they are a warning to all, vengeance will materialize to anyone who assails me.'

"Stepping back into my mind, I tried to decide how to respond. But before I could, the new day's sunlight caught the corner of my eye as it peeked over the Earth. I raised my hand, trying to shade the light from my eyes, but as I did the man vanished. Alone, I was left with nothing but an odd curiosity and words spoken to me in my head, 'I could give you forever, away from this life.'

"I went to the stables to begin my work for the day, not knowing what to think of the man. I tried to spend the day thinking of other things. After I was done attending to the horses, I returned home without a word spoken to my parents about the odd man. The last thing I had heard that morning, the alluring sentence, continued to ring in my ears.

"I could have forever, away from this life. I thought as I lay in bed staring up at the ceiling, What could that mean? It had to be better than my current situation. I did not make enough money to arrange a marriage and rarely had contact with people, just horses. Maybe it was a needed change."

Jack's Diary

My king is my maker and my master.

Jack Year 0 Day 1 AV

"The next morning, hours before the sun shone upon the city, I went out to the perimeter wall looking for the muscular man. The moon was shrouded in a cape of storm clouds, leaving me to walk blindly along the wall in hopes of hearing the voice in my head again. The cool breeze easily penetrated the woolen cloak that I had put on to defend from the chill. It was an ominous sign that fell on my deaf ears. I felt as though I were searching for evil to make a deal with the devil, but the unhappiness of my daily situation drove me to continue.

"Eventually, something moved in front of me. In the darkness of the night, I had no ability to discern what it was and assumed the worst. Fumbling for my dagger, I threw my arm out in front of me to block the enemy, but before I could get the knife out of its holster, a voice invaded my mind. 'You have returned. May I assume you were tempted by my offer of eternal life?'

"I had no response to this. I knew I could not pass

up that kind of opportunity, but I was too terrified to do anything. I could only stare out into the void of night.

"Minutes passed with no sound other than the emptiness of the wind when he emerged from his invisibility of the shadows and put his hands on my shoulders. 'You may live forever. I only ask you to support me on occasion and fulfill your destiny by conceding to my wishes. You will need to tell me yes or no.'

"Suddenly, a piercing pain came to my throat. I felt as if a boar had mistaken my neck for food. The mysterious man's hands clawed into my shoulders, ripping the flesh and soaking my cloak with my own blood. Out of desperation, I croaked out to the darkness, 'Yes! If it will make you stop, yes!'

"He dropped me. I collapsed on the ground. The pain remained for a while, but eventually, I felt my youth and vigor return. As the morning approached, I was led up the hill toward the castle. The sun had not yet risen, but I could see clearer than I ever could at midday. The castle was an amazing sight in the darkness, standing perfectly still as a monument to man and time.

"He led me into the castle, past the guards, and into the royal chambers. In shock, I looked to the man for assurance, hoping he was a servant and not an assassin. He slowly stepped toward me and reached out a hand. 'I did not want to tell you until I knew your true motives… I am King Eden, the lord over all that lands within the city's walls.' He spoke with nobility and a much deeper voice than I had been hearing in my head.

"Immediately, I bowed to my king in repentance for thinking he was an evil murderer. The king smiled at the submission to his will and helped me back to my feet. It was from there that the king took me under his wing. I learned everything I needed to know about vampirism and in return, I acted as his mercenary. For a hundred years, we lived within the kingdom. He ruled over the citizens and I slayed the enemies of my king.

"We spent years after that in London, Africa, here in the New World… And everywhere we have gone, he has given me everything I need and I smite the supporters of his enemies. You, unfortunately, well, I don't know how you fit in."

Known Vampiric Biology

As a species, they appear to not be vulnerable to injury. Wounds tend to heal. Breathing is unnecessary. Only severed limbs appear to be permanent.

Jack Year 1610 Day 84 AV

"Did you say we are immortal?" Thomas was in absolute astonishment. He felt like he had superpowers when he ran sixty miles an hour or when he would jump fifty feet into the air, but to be undead, that seemed impossible.

Jack saw the glint of mischief growing in Thomas's eye and he felt it important to squelch it before it got out of hand. "I wouldn't call it immortality. Yes, we are incredibly powerful, feel almost no pain and recover instantaneously, but…" Jack continued with extreme caution, "you can die."

Thomas was growing impatient. He felt Jack was being blatantly deceptive. "So, how can I die? You said yourself that I basically can't get hurt." Thomas, still sitting in the green sludge of the sewers, hit the waters, creating a small splash as if he were a four year old not getting his way.

"A severed limb will not heal unless it is held together while you heal. So, the only real fear any of us have is decapitation." Jack kept looking into the water in the center of the room as if he expected it to speak to him. His mannerisms were becoming less animated and his voice grew softer.

Thomas looked at him thinking that decapitation was not exactly an everyday occurrence. Jack might have well said they were immortal. He wanted to ask about religion, but he barely got the word "God" out of his mouth before Jack frantically waved his hands, trying to get Thomas to stop talking.

Jack was visibly concerned now, with his eyes opened to their full potential. He began to climb the ladder out of the sewer and called back to Thomas when he was halfway to surface, "It is almost sunup. You need to get back."

Thomas, confused by Jack's behavior, followed suit and climbed the steel ladder. As he pushed off the last piece of steel rebar that was the final rung of the ladder, he looked out at the world and noticed that he still had at least an hour before the sun returned. He climbed fully out of the manhole and replaced the cover over the round opening.

Looking to each side, he saw nothing but the normality for the street. The church sat in front of him with the office buildings and community center to each side with a few crows dabbled about. He looked up to soak in some of the moon's energy when he noticed Jack was perched atop the old church, looking like a gargoyle overlooking the entrance to God's house.

It only took one thrust from his thighs and calves for

Thomas to reach the crown of the church. He slipped as he maneuvered the steep roof over the tall worship hall. Then he looked over at Jack and asked, "What was that about?"

Jack stared at the manhole cover. "You must be careful about what you say." He paused for a second then continued. "And who hears you."

Many questions were swirling around Thomas's mind, but he could not separate them out. He decided to go back to his theme, thinking that Jack was trying to throw him off. "What about God?" Thomas overemphasized the word.

"It should not be thought." Jack considered stopping there, but the frustration erupting on Thomas's face told him to continue. "There are certain things a vampire does not do." He did not want to say it and he tried to use telepathy to tell Thomas, but it was not working. Finally, exasperated, he said aloud, "We have no soul. We can not go to heaven. We have no dedication to God." Jack stared into the Thomas's face looking for acceptance or rejection.

Thomas should have been worried, but his faith was unwavering. He brushed it off like it was no big deal. "You're wrong. We do have a soul. God would not have sent you if we didn't have a soul."

Jack heard the words come out of Thomas's mouth, but he could not believe them. A thousand-plus years as a vampire had taught him that saying something like that was a cardinal sin. He refocused his attention on the manhole cover in the street and waited for Thomas to elaborate, letting the fear build up in his throat as if he were being strangled.

Thomas noticed Jack returning to his statuesque state so he continued to explain. "What are the odds that you, a vampire who only feeds on the dead, would feed on me when I was in a room with two dead people? What are the odds that I could not will myself to move? What are the odds that I would see purpose in my life as soon as I was bit by a vampire when I had never felt religion in my life before? God has called upon me. You were sent to me by God to give me the power to cleanse the world of a type of sinner. I am an angel, a messenger of God, created to rid the world of thieves."

Thomas continued by stating the Ten Commandments, but Jack had tuned out. He had never heard a vampire speak that way. It was uplifting and created a small twinge of hope in his heart thinking they could be angels with a greater purpose than they knew, but Jack knew the truth. There was no reality in the drivel Thomas was spouting. All he knew was Thomas needed to stop saying these things before he brought hell to Earth. He asserted himself a little more and continued with what he felt he needed to say to the new vampire.

"Be careful what you do and say. I learned a lot over the years. There is a reason why I feed off the dead. If you keep feeding and dumping your leftovers all over town, getting in the news and having police reports on you. You will have your hands full."

"Are you threatening me?" Thomas was on his feet atop the church ready for a physical confrontation with Jack.

"No. I don't mean with me or the police, for that matter. There are other vampires that don't want attention brought to the fact that they exist. They don't want you in the public eye. So, be careful and inconspicuous. And…" Jack trailed off trying to find the words. "I wouldn't be talking about your pact with God if I were you." He whispered the word "God" while he looked over his shoulder at the gathering murder of crows on the recreation center.

Thomas stared down at Jack, crouched at the edge of the church, still staring at the manhole in the street. "I am here to serve God, to follow his will, to spread the Word. This is my calling in life and you can't say anything to change my beliefs."

Jack felt the sun burn into his scalp as it emerged in the distance. He was terrified. Not of Thomas's speech, but of the conviction that he held and the consequences Jack knew would come. It had to be the man he brought into the covenant. He had no time to contemplate as the sun was showing itself for the beginning of the day and boring into his skin. He leapt off the roof of the church, landing in the center of the street. Tearing the manhole cover out of the ground, he slithered into the sewer and sent Thomas a telepathic message. I hope you rethink this, but I will keep it to myself for now.

Thomas heard the message run through his head. He began to wonder who Jack could possibly talk to about this, but before he came to any conclusions, the sun sapped his energy and he fell off the roof of the church. Landing in the shade of the building, he decided it was time to get inside before he was weakened to a burning lump of mush.

Jack sat below the surface of the city, allowing Thomas's infernal thoughts infect his mind. He tried to drive them out, but it was no use. Nothing could get the hope out of his mind. Sitting in the muck of the sewer, he tried to disguise his identity, creating characters in his head that might throw the spy off. The last thing he needed was to be accused of worship.

He eyed the manhole cover, knowing that just outside of that iron disc lay a sanctuary where his mind could not be invaded, but someone would see him enter. If he could brave the sunlight, avoid the witness of the crow, and make his way into the church, he would be safe to let his mind wander anywhere he liked, but that was all a fantasy. It might be a fantasy that brought him to conviction by the unearthly father.

Jack crawled down one of the tubes away from the center point of the city. He knew that he could not escape the mind infiltration, but away from the main room of the city's entrails he could let something slip out of his mouth. No one would hear him if he were out journeying the sewage system.

The ribbed steel tubes brought no comfort to Jack, still unable to think about the forbidden. Wandering the tunnels was just confirmation that he was a vampire and there was no out for him. He returned to the main room, all the while telling himself that he could not go to the church. It was full of lies. His belief did not agree with his thoughts, but he ran the ideas through his head to convince anyone listening to his thoughts that he was loyal to the clan.

Known Vampiric Biology

Vampires have highly advanced senses.

Thomas Year 1 Day 52 AV

It was a Sunday and Thomas was lying in darkness. The cellar filled with a perfect void in his sight, a sensation he no longer experienced anywhere but the church.

A lot of thought had been put into the strange sensations that took place within the church. Overall, Thomas felt like he was still in his old life when he was there. Down in the cellar, he could not see in the dark or hear from a distance. His vision in the worship hall was clear, lacking the normal color blur that haunted his normal days. The only remaining reminders of his vampiric biology was not having to breathe and the inability to sleep. Other than those, he would have thought he was a human.

A recurring thought plagued Thomas. He did not understand why he was experiencing what he was. He waved his hand in front of his face, but the darkness of the basement left it completely invisible. Staring out at nothing, but knowing something was there, reminded him of his relationship with God. Was God protecting him? Was the building truly a sanctuary so Thomas would not be forced to accept the unavoidable reality? It was too much to contemplate.

He heard steps going up the stairs. Each creak echoing into the small cell of a room was proof that Lilith was climbing out into the worship hall. As the door opened momentarily, a shine from the world above him glimmered in. Thomas could hear the organ playing a verse of Ava Maria, but just as quickly as these sensations came into the room, they disappeared. Lilith had shut the door.

Thomas had been staying at the church for well over a year, and he still had never spoken to Lilith. He was flabbergasted by the unspoken relationship between the two of them. He was constantly misreading it as puppy love, but it was much more than that. Whether it was a long lost sibling or a friend from a past life he did not know. He just felt a connection to her. It was not a sexual tension but more like someone you would trust with your life, someone you would sacrifice for, but someone you just want acceptance from. It was something that Thomas had never had before. His resentment toward his brothers left that relationship damaged. Thomas's misinterpretation of his parents' affection snubbed their bond early on. But with no verbal contact, Thomas finally felt the intimate connection with Lilith, a complete stranger.

He did not attribute it at the time, but his heightened senses and his ability to feel people's moods and emotions are what built the connection. Thomas had been able to understand people's every move, but since his only contact with Lilith had been inside the church, she remained the beautiful mystery that he so desperately yearned to solve.

Thomas knew it was still early in the morning, but he felt the need to go upstairs and witness the church ceremony as it unfolded. His long tenure at the church had not yet included a church service, but he wanted to rectify that. He slowly rose to an upright position on his cot, not bending any part of his body except his hips, a stereotypical vampire move. After looking like a 1950s horror movie vampire waking up from his coffin sleep, he turned to get out of bed. His feet, which no longer were covered by shoes, pressed against the cold cement floor and pushed his body upright to exit the room.

He shuffled warily across the floor, trying not to bump into the other cots in the perfect darkness as he made his way to the stairway. As he pushed his never-slumbering body up the stairwell, the faint sound of the church organ teased his ears. Upon opening the door and climbing out of his hole, the light in the room nearly blinded him and tried to send him back down into the depths of the basement. But he refused to let it get to him.

Once he got past the initial shock of the light, the room was its own magnificent splendor. The first three rows of pews had begun to fill with people kneeling with their eyes closed, trying to direct the attention of God to their personal cause. The glorious music pouring out of the organ danced throughout the majestic hall, bringing a sense of peace to the parishioners.

Thomas quietly stepped out from the side of the altar where the stairs appeared. Trying to be stealthy, he quickly heel-toed his steps to get to the pews. The realization that he was not very graceful when he was not dodging life in the shadows of night hit him like a hammer to the face. He considered running to the back where he could lock himself in the bathroom to execute his normal bathing technique involving paper towels and the sink, but felt that he might miss the beginning of the rite. As he slid into the last pew and bowed his head, paying respects to Christ, he sat in the sunlit room free from his vampiric pains of the light.

As the light beamed in through the few windows of the building, he looked at his pale skin in the natural radiance of day. He had become so pale that he had surpassed the white of paper and had entered a more translucent appearance. He could see his veins and the gore of his internal flesh through the skin. He felt as though his skin were getting thinner and was more like that of a balloon, barely separating his internal self from the devastating conditions of the outside world.

The hideousness of his arm left him afraid of how terrifying his face must look. He pictured talking to a stranger on the street and them looking at how his muscles moved in his face with his vampiric life source pumping through the veins in his visage. It even gave him chills.

The parishioners eventually filled the room. All but the last few pews were full. Thomas was left as the sole inhabitant of the final pew. The music began and the entire room rose to their feet to observe the entrance of the Holy Gospel carried by Father Timeus. Watching the sea of people wave to their feet in unison was credit to the power of the Bible itself. It was a tradition that had lasted well beyond the memory of any person, family, or traceable genealogy. He got to his feet, in respect of the tradition.

Once Thomas had joined the rest of the room on his feet, he noticed one person who remained seated. Her dark hair and her shoulder blades protruding from the back of her spaghetti strap dress told Thomas it was Lilith. She remained seated, leaning forward with her hands clasped and pressed against her forehead. She cringed in anguish as she silently pleaded with God.

When the priest entered through the back door holding the Bible over his head, the members of the church exploded in song. Timeus slowly walked down the center aisle while rhythmic chanting surrounded him.

Thomas felt energized from the experience. The tradition felt unchanged from a thousand years before. It was incredible to experience a ritual that had remained considerably intact for so long. Passion and happiness flowed throughout Thomas's body as the ceremony continued. It was during the Peace, when the parishioners turn to each other and allow a chorus of "Peace be with you" echo all over the hall, that Thomas began to wonder about Jack. He could not understand why he would not come inside the church. The fear the old vampire seemed to harbor for the rest of his unseen community did not feel appropriate to his lifespan, experience, and powers.

The ceremony continued, with the mass of the people rotating between sitting, kneeling, or standing in a pattern that was mysterious to Thomas. Eventually, everyone returned to sitting and the priest took the podium to give his sermon.

He read from the book of Genesis. At first, Thomas let his mind drift, not listening to the words booming around the great building. He looked at a painting of Christ being crucified which hung from the wall behind the pews. The image was quite gruesome with the thorns piercing into Jesus' face, blood streaming down into his eyes. Nails punctured his wrists, causing what appeared to be a very painful dislocation of the hands. But it was the pigment of Christ's arm that held Thomas's attention. It was an opaque white, not identical to Thomas's, but similar.

After staring into the painting for a couple of minutes, Thomas turned back and looked at his own hands. He envisioned his wrists being nailed to a cross while being persecuted by the vampire population. This was a common ground he shared with the son of God, martyred by a society he did not know for a society he no longer belonged to. He wanted to stand and shout that he had given his life for the well-being of others in honor of God and his son, but it was not appropriate. He felt alone. He tried to push these ideas out of his head and focus on the sermon.

Thomas was treated to the story of Cain and Abel.

The story explained how Abel sacrificed the firstborn of his herd to God while Cain sacrificed some of the edges of his crops. This struck a chord with him. He felt he was giving to God by working as a vampire, while the majority of the people in the room were there to prove their belief system to themselves. It was just in the same way Abel gave substantially of his work while Cain seemed to sacrifice just the edges to appease the law of God. He looked up to see that there were very few people even listening to the sermon now. They were just fidgeting and looking to kill time. He again felt alone.

The story went on as God accepted Abel's offering and rejected Cain's. In the end, Cain killed his brother and was banished from Eden by the Creator and forced to wander through the land of Nod, where he would bear a mark to protect him from people trying to avenge Abel and their deity. Thomas felt the tragedy of the story and related to the actions of God. He felt God's retribution for the ancient hate crime just as he felt God's vengeance on those who disobeyed the eighth commandment. But he did not understand why he was the one who was banished to Nod, not able to emerge during the day, seeking food as a scavenger of the sinners. He was the holy one in the modern Bible story. Why had the two robbers not been forced to an eternity of limbo while he was given the everlasting kingdom of heaven? He felt he bore the burden of both men. He felt even more alone.

As the sermon delved into the meaning and purpose of the passages, Thomas noticed Lilith again from the corner of his eye. She was still shaking with her hands clasped together, praying. She rocked back and forth ever so slightly as tears dripped from her eyes down onto her dress. The pain she displayed across her weathered face left Thomas wanting to hold her and comfort her from the unjust torture of life. He did not know why she was upset, but he could physically feel the desire to help her. Without knowing what her baggage was, he tried to comfort her telepathically. It did not appear to change anything.

People a few pews up from Thomas got up to go to the front of the church and receive communion. It seemed an odd ritual to him. He could not grasp the idea that the bread and the wine were actually the body and blood of Christ. The parishioners stood in line for their turn to drink from the golden goblet and have a paper-thin bread wafer placed on their tongue.

"The body of Christ, the bread of heaven," Father Timeus said as he placed the bread in the people's hands or straight into their mouths, depending on their posture. On the other side of the altar, the members of the church kneeled before another priest who said, "The blood of Christ, the cup of salvation."

He sat back and watched as each person closed their eyes to take Christ into their body, most of them not understanding the weight of what they were doing. He wondered how many of the people at the front had actually considered what the priests were saying. Did they believe that they were receiving Christ in a physical way, as if they had drained his blood and served his flesh?

The last of the people got to the front of the church for their serving of the savior. Lilith had not gone up. Thomas looked over at her pew and she remained quivering in intense prayer. He strained his mind trying to help her, but in the end, he felt there was nothing he could do.

He remained in his seat, watching the woman he was infatuated with sob uncontrollably. The songs, the sitting, the standing, the kneeling all seemed insignificant as his gaze refused to break from Lilith. The perfection of her beauty, the true form of the human structure, an exquisiteness that could only be derived from truly experiencing life was contrasted with the weakness that she could not hide from inside her barest self.

He sat there and stared until the service ended and Father Timeus came over to help her to his office. Thomas looked up at the Pearly Gates-stained glass window and realized although he attended church, he did not pray. He felt better and more spiritual, but that morning, there was no conversation with his Lord.

Thomas rummaged through the bin of clothing the priest had suggested he shop from. After the church ceremony, Father Timeus was left with the difficult task of explaining to the vampire that he would always be welcome during service, but he did not want him to discourage others from worship.

The clothes Thomas had been wearing were the same work clothes that he changed into his vampiric state in. Of course, he washed them in the sink of the church on a semi-daily basis, but they bore holes that exposed unsightly flesh and they carried a stench within them that was not pleasant.

The choice of clothing Thomas was left with was not great. The bin was donated to the church by parishioners who felt the organization could deliver it to the neediest. Thomas apparently fit that description.

His shoes had completely worn away and for the past month, he had been going barefoot while his pants continuously got shorter and his shirt thinner. Although he would not previously been caught dead in any of the items now at his disposal, he decided being caught undead in them was all right.

He took a couple pairs of tennis shoes along with one pair of dress shoes. Unfortunately, there were only white socks, leaving Thomas with a Michael Jacksonesque set of pedal apparel.

He sadly tossed his old work shirt in the garbage as he replaced his wardrobe for the rest of his body with light clothing in an attempt to avoid contrast with his opaque skin.

He was grateful for the gifts and the fresh set of clothes as he parted with the last remnants of his former self.

Timeus watched the shopping spree from the doorway, trying to convince himself that Thomas was not an evil spirit. He gave him the clothes in an attempt to love his neighbor, but by the time he gave it to him, it was to keep his parish from losing part of its congregation.

He watched the vampire rummage and could see the parallel to the redheaded boy he killed so many years ago, but there was no lesson learned. He still just wanted the man to leave him alone and never return to damage his world. If he could drive out Thomas without having to do the physical labor, he would, but he did not know how to do it.

Daily Examiner

Wednesday morning there was another victim of the Embalming Killer found. The victim was left in the middle of Mulgrove Street during the late hours of the night.

Thomas Year 1 Day 118 AV

Atop the city library, peering out from behind a statue of a great poet, Thomas watched as the police investigated one of his feedings. They stared at the body of the vile mugger/rapist and questioned the motives of the dead criminal's attacker.

Thomas lay his head on the shoulder of Milton. He wanted to say, "I can tell you why! I could make you understand." He could have described in detail the purse that the man stole and then after not finding any money, came back for some carnal payback. He wanted to scream it from the rooftop, but he knew better.

The police continued their investigation, putting little markers on the body then on the ground. They searched the asphalt looking for clues while Thomas laughed to himself. He knew that they would find nothing. He did not kill the man in the middle of the street. He was put there as an example for all the other sinners. The cops would have to travel across town to find the location of the incident.

"It's another one. Looks like he has been drained of his blood too," said a short, fat cop referring to past feeding victims of Thomas. The man pushed his uniform to its limits with the stitching and buttons holding on to the fabric like a cat dangling over a bathtub. He waddled when he walked and always had a bit of spittle in the corner of his mouth, something the other police officers seemed to try to avoid direct eye contact with.

An older, but more fit officer replied, "I don't know how the Embalming Killer does it. There is absolutely no exit wound. Where does he drain the blood from?"

Thomas, listening with his extremely sensitive hearing, found the serial killer name amusing, but wished they understood his purpose. Maybe they would call him the Righteous Killer. It felt more fitting to him.

The police continued their search, looking for fingerprints and DNA samples. They did the same routine with each one of Thomas's feedings that they found. It was more a futile exercise of policy since they knew it was another murder of the "Embalming Killer." Nevertheless, they continued their investigation just as they had been taught, only witnessed by Thomas and a stray crow flying around the crime scene.

Thomas wanted to run down to them and explain. It was driving him crazy witnessing the dusting of light poles and photographing oil spots in the street. He wished they could see the crosses he carved into the body, but his vampiric venom healed those wounds. He wished they would notice the man was placed lying on top of his hands to signify his thievery just as if he were to cut the hands from the carcass, but he was expecting too much. These were not the police of the prime-time dramas. These were real cops that did not finish college, that were on the verge of becoming criminals themselves, the type of people who would rather see a man get beaten because he was a prick than to understand why he did what he did. These men were never going to understand Thomas unless it was spelled out for them.

One of the officers pulled out his laptop from his cruiser. They all gathered round the computer to look at pictures from Thomas's other feedings. They stared into the screen looking at debris, which happened to be around the sites where he dumped bodies, trying to find some sort of clues.

The cops were baffled by this specific killing since all the others showed up in a specific dumpster with the same lack of blood and no breaks in the skin. This time, however, it was in the middle of a street. They considered the idea that the killer was getting sloppy, that he felt he was uncatchable, but again, it was pure speculation.

Thomas watched for an hour, laughing at how they could not figure out why this body was different. Was it special somehow? Was this murder not trash like the rest? Was this one supposed to sit in the open for a reason? They considered the possibility of a copycat killer, which had Thomas almost rolling on the roof in hysterics. Maybe they thought they were the prime-time drama cops, but Thomas knew better.

Eventually, he lay down on the roof, feeling the cool air of the fall night, staring up at the moon in relaxation. He was pulling energy from the lunar rock when a familiar face came into view and blocked the moon's beams.

"Did I not show you how to get rid of bodies so no one would find them?" Jack had a scowl across his face, showing his obvious displeasure about the scene unfolding in the street. Thomas just smirked at Jack, feeling he simply did not understand that this was God's will. Jack spoke up again. "You will be in the papers tomorrow and certain vampires will not be happy."

"What is going to happen? We are immortal, remember?" Thomas was taking a sarcastic tone with Jack, which did not make Jack happy.

"If they figure this out, which they will once they get past the superstitions, then all vampires all over the world will have to go back into hiding. And you, my friend…" Jack let an evil grin emerge on his lips, "you may just lose your head if we all have to go back into hiding."

Thomas felt Jack was lobbing idle threats, but was slightly concerned with the insinuation that vampires had been in hiding before. "Why would we hide? Who is going to take us on?"

Jack was gritting his teeth, chipping off tiny pieces of

them, not realizing the amount of muscle he was pouring into his frustration. "Have you never heard of a witch hunt? Maybe the Salem witch trials? The Council of Paderborn? The Inquisition? North Berwick Trials? These aren't folklore; these things happened. You better not think that just because you are a vampire now that you can change the whole system. It will end with all of us hiding in a cave for a hundred years and your head on a post." Jack was so furious he was almost growling as his teeth regenerated from his previous teeth-grinding episode.

Thomas held back a little with the sarcasm, but wanted to express what he was thinking. He took a quick look over his shoulder to see that the police were still down in the street, now bagging the victim, preparing to take him to the morgue. When he turned back, Jack's white eyes were piercing Thomas's confidence. "If you would just understand that God gave me…"

Jack cut him off. "You think this is a gift from God? You think this is a miracle? You haven't had this burden long enough to realize it is a curse. I have been trying to protect you, but you won't shut up about God!" Jack walked over to the edge of the library, looking down at the police finishing their investigation.

Thomas was treading softly in order to not push Jack to the breaking point. "I have been given the opportunity to save humanity from what did me in. I should have been killed or imprisoned after a robbery at my job. You keep saying everlasting life is a curse, but so are freewill, evil, and empathy. I owe my new life to God. If I shouldn't give my life to him, who should I dedicate it to?"

Jack, still furious, was only half-listening but retorted nonetheless. "God did not give you an opportunity. My ignorance gave you this chance. It isn't an opportunity at all. What you fail to address is the fact that because I made a mistake and because of me, you have no soul!"

Jack watched the police drive away, leaving the street abandoned like a normal four-in-the-morning day. He turned back to Thomas and just before he hopped backward off the building, he said, "I don't care who you dedicate this nonlife to, but if you give it to God, you will be sorry." The threat was for show as Jack wanted to believe Thomas, but due to his circumstance, he had to oppose him.

Thomas watched Jack fall off the library and scamper into the sewers the moment he hit. The sight reminded him of a snake slithering away after it took its prey. Thomas was left on the roof, energized by the moon and dumbstruck by Jack's rebuttal. He did not understand why Jack believed they were soulless creatures just wandering with no purpose. He felt it was obvious he had a purpose, more obvious than it was while he was human.

He walked over to the edge of the building and began running from roof to roof. Jumping through the obscurity, unnoticed by the people below, he prolonged his thoughts about Jack's words.

Why was he so against God? It was not that he did not believe in God, but he was vehemently anti-Christian.

Nothing made more sense than the idea that he hated his life and held God accountable. Then why would he want Thomas to stop talking about it? He decided there must be something he was missing.

Thomas looked around to see where he ended up. He had been on autopilot, allowing his body to guide him while his thoughts ran their own course. He was in front of the church, looking at its bland exterior, but he was not going inside. He had stopped just to the side of the manhole cover as if he were heading down into the sewers. He thought it was odd that his body led him there almost as if he were drawn to it. He brushed it off and decided to go back into the church. Although it was not light out yet, it was not early in the night either.

With his head drooped down, Thomas stared at the ground as he walked back to his home. His feet, forced into shoes three sizes too small, which would have brought a normal man to his knees in painful blisters, gave him no sensation. He tried to take a deep breath and again, no sensation. He touched the oak door to the church and still no sensation.

He thought for a minute about what Jack had said and considered that maybe it is a curse to be a vampire. He could not feel anything anymore. Then as he crossed the threshold of the church, he could feel the old wooden pews with his hand as he passed them, the air felt crisp from the air conditioner, and the doors felt rough from wear. Then he realized that God was there for him. God had given him a gift and when he was in God's house, he was treated as all of God's other creations.

Known Vampiric Biology

The creatures can not hold pigmentation in their skin or eyes. Their entire existence is a constant dispelling of their pigmentation.

Thomas Year 2 Day 25 AV

Lilith stood at the back of the church leaning over the water basin. She splashed her face with the holy water, hoping to receive some holy relief through the water. The basin was four feet tall, made out of cherry wood, adorned with images of Christ on the cross on all four sides. The top held the small silver bowl that was half-full of water reflecting Lilith's grotesquely thin image in its sides.

She bowed her head and prayed her usual prayer while supporting herself by holding each hand onto the sides of the basin. The flicker of the candlelit chandeliers created the illusion of her shaking as she hovered over the bowl. Her elbows protruded from her skin, showing all of the knobs that made up the joint. She was weak from lack of food, but she was not sure if she wanted to eat or not.

Thomas watched her as he made his way from the top of the stairs to where she was standing. He felt the nerves of a young boy getting the chance to talk for the first time to the girl he adored. He had been at the church for nearly two years and this would be the first time he spoke to her. Each step took him closer to the encounter he had been yearning over nearly his entire vampiric existence. It, unfortunately, was to be nothing more than a professional meeting.

He reached to tap her on the shoulder and she jumped, not expecting the touch, as she turned around. The momentum of her leap caused her shirt to fly up a little bit, revealing the detail of her lower ribs, perfectly shading her concaved stomach, looking emaciated beyond repair. Landing on her feet and slightly leaning back, supported by her hands now on opposite sides of the basin, she panted in shock. Her shorts hung from her hips, engulfing her near fat-and-muscle-less legs.

"I'm sorry to startle you. Father Timeus had suggested we talk." Thomas tried to be as formal and nonaggressive as possible. "I am Thomas." He extended his right hand for pleasantries. The unsheathed arm hung in the air, exposing his complexion of near decay.

Lilith was apprehensive about his appearance. She had seen him around the church every now and then, but never a close-up look at the man. His lack of pigmentation was enough to unsettle her stomach, but if the priest had suggested they meet, then she felt she needed to work through it. She put out her still-wet hand and softly grasped his.

They retreated to a pew where Thomas sat down while staring at Lilith's anorexic figure. Lilith did the same, slightly repulsed by Thomas's earthworm complexion. They faced each other, Lilith noticing Thomas's sharp teeth. She silently in her head questioned his humanity.

They both assumed that their meeting was to be a type of peer counseling session and Lilith decided to take the lead and ask what brought Thomas to the church.

"So?" Lilith spoke just to break the silence. "What brought you here?"

"I am doing the work of God." He wanted to leave it at that. The last thing he wanted was to scare her away. She tilted her head to the side, appearing like an innocent five year old and waited for more.

"A couple of years ago, I found myself homeless and lost. I happened upon Father Timeus and his church. It is a sign from God that I am here to please him and not live by material gains. So, I am staying here and spreading the Word of God." Thomas ceased his miniature speech and hoped that it would satisfy Lilith's question. Unfortunately, she did not say anything. Her sunken cheeks and protruding cheekbones froze in time, waiting for him to continue his story.

The flicker of the light in her eyes reflected on the internal shield she wielded. Thomas could feel her pain seething from within her regardless of the wall she hid behind so people would not judge her. Watching her watch him, he felt a burning desire to change the subject.

"I'm sorry to be so intrusive, but I've seen you crying at mass many times." As soon as the words left his lips, he regretted it. He wished he could reach out and pluck them out of the air and hide them back down into his gut.

Lilith was shocked at the nerve of this man. She had known of him for a long time, but this, the first time they spoke, he questions her emotional state. She wanted to stomp out of the room, stomp on his heart, or stomp his existence away from hers, but again, she felt if Father Timeus wanted them to speak she should honor that request. She had received so much from the church that she tried to respect anything the priest sent her way. "It was nothing." She tried to lead him away from the subject.

"Are you sure? It seemed so troubling." Thomas ignored her attempt to move on.

"Really, I am fine. I am only trying to get back on my feet." She swallowed hard in an attempt to keep down the lump in her throat.

"Father Timeus seems to think we can help each other. Please, every time I see you so upset I just want to know how I can help. The pain you are feeling at those times should not be felt by any person. Your soul has been trying to reach out to me. Please let it."

The innocence she was using to mask her emotions faded and a face full of pain and hatred surfaced. Thomas watched as a beautiful creature turned her faith to her exterior and began to spew forth her tribulation. "OK."

She bowed her head, staring at the floor, the same posture she held the first time Thomas saw her talking to the priest. "I should be used to talking about this by now, but for some reason, just thinking about it makes me nauseous. I was told as time went by it would get easier, but that's just not true." She bent forward on the pew, leaning in toward Thomas. Her hands clasped together, creating obvious strain in her arms. Thomas looked down at her hands and noticed that tears had begun to fall on them. Her breath became erratic as she began weeping. "My son died three years ago."

Thomas felt his heart drop, as this was something he could not understand. He had no children and did not appreciate his relationship with his parents. He bobbed his head faintly as Lilith continued. "The father had left and I was all alone in the city, just me and Amon, my son. He was a year old and the light of my life. I could watch him all day, learning to walk and making these adorable little babbling sounds. It's funny, I was always worried about living in the bad part of town, but I had no money so we were in a slum, an all-bills-paid kind of place. But we were never endangered from that." Lilith let a small smile shine through her tears of her loss, but with her head down it was hidden from Thomas.

She bit her bottom lip in preparation for what she was about to say. "He got sick." The words were quiet but more powerful than any three-word sentence Thomas had ever heard. She emitted years of love, pain, and regret with three syllables. She stopped for a minute or two, trying to hold down the anguish.

"I thought it was nothing. A cold or a virus, but he seemed OK." Her words were barely distinguishable through the sobbing. "We went to bed that night and that was it. He never woke up. It was the worst day of my life and I can't stop reliving it." She crumpled into the pew. The process of actually saying the words converted her trickle of tears into a river of grief.

Thomas rubbed her back while she continued to crumble before his eyes. There was nothing he could do for her other than sitting in silence, respecting her emotions. Finally, her tears relented to a bearable pace, an opportunity she seized to finish what she was telling Thomas.

"Now he would be four. I never got to see him learn to talk, start riding a bicycle, prepare for school. In just one year, my life was taken from me. This beautiful boy was ripped from my love just as I was coming into my own as a mother. I wake up in the morning hoping to see his face smiling back at me, but it never happens. I just want to see him and be with him."

The air between the two was awkward. Thomas had no answer to give Lilith relief so he opened his mouth and let nature take over. "I am sorry you had to go through that, but God has a plan. It may seem inhumane now, but he has a plan for you. As painful as your life may be, you will see him again. When you reach heaven, he will be there for you. Don't hold a grudge against God or man..." Thomas was cut off by Lilith.

"I don't hate God. I just miss my son. I could be bitter and hate him for it, but I understand that I was asked to sacrifice. I don't know why, but it happened. If I hated God, I would have killed myself years ago. I just want to be able to be happy again."

"Do you ever go a day without thinking of him?"

"No, and I don't want to. I will never forget him. But I would like to be able to remember him and not feel the devastation of my loss. I would love to sit down and tell someone how great it was to be around him, but I can't because all I can do is hurt." Lilith pulled herself up from the seat of the pew and leaned on Thomas's shoulder. This was the first time she touched him without thinking about his appearance.

Thomas was torn. He felt her pain, but was enthralled that she was touching him. The fact that she was confiding in him and seeking comfort through his touch meant the world to him.

His infatuation with her had grown as he delved into her psyche and her view of God after such a horrific experience. Here was someone who had been through so much and had every reason to resent God and yet, was still worshipping him and trying to live a good life. He thought if more people could have her view of the planet, God may not need him to eradicate thieves.

Lilith picked up her head, leaving a small damp spot on Thomas's recycled yet dingy shirt. She looked up into his colorless eyes with an appreciation she could not have held when she first laid eyes upon him. "Thank you. I think it helps to talk." She pulled her head up as if she contemplated kissing him, but he turned away.

Thomas questioned the relationship they were building. He felt as though it should not be sexual or lustful in any way as if that would be taking advantage of a broken and vulnerable woman, but she appeared to disagree. Inside the church, without the ability to feel her thoughts, he misinterpreted her desire as she had intended to kiss him, but only in appreciation for what he had done for her.

She got to her feet, tears still flowing, but at a manageable rate, holding Thomas's cold hand, she told him that she was tired and needed to go to sleep for the night. As she made her way to the stairs, she turned back to Thomas, her hair dangling in her face, all the muscles of her neck tensing, looking as if cables lay under the skin of her neck. She said, "I hope we can talk again." Then she descended the stairs into the cellar.

Her head disappeared beneath the floor and Thomas reflected on her as a person. Her pain touched him, her view of God uplifted him, and her life experience made her that much more beautiful. His first impressions of her did not compare to the perfection that she actually embodied.

Jack's Diary

I am thinking about letting him win.

Thomas Year 2 Day 26 AV

The air rushed by Thomas's head as he sped over the rooftops at over seventy miles an hour. He was in close pursuit of Jack. He knew he could catch him if he just pushed a little harder. Running was a different task than it was before he became a vampire. He no longer tried to make his legs go as fast as possible, but instead, tried to push off with each leg as hard as possible. It was more like the triple jump except the number of jumps just kept rising.

Thomas stumbled as he took a step early in his stride after noticing his pace had him set to land in a gorge in between buildings. One step, two steps, next building. One step, two steps, next building. One step, next building. He felt his pace increase watching Jack, his target, dart away, but he was not letting him get away. He looked up to see the center of town and realized that they were about to take an abrupt left turn.

Thomas planted his right foot and pushed off to the left. Soaring through the air with his left foot held out to catch the pavement below, Thomas missed the long lost sensation of falling, the rush he used to get when on a roller coaster. The fleeting memories of falling were replaced by a near panic when Thomas realized he had landed on a freeway and was feet away from an oncoming car. He threw all of his weight to the side to avoid the car, landing in the weeds of the median.

Jack was already bouncing down the street. Thomas hopped back to his feet and took off again. He was fuming at his misstep. There was almost no way he would catch Jack in time now. He took a chance and jumped onto a moving car, then leapt off it, trying to steal a little of the car's momentum, but before he could use his newfound speed, Jack turned off the expected path into a city park. Thomas, on his trail, followed, dodging in between trees and avoiding walking pedestrians. He saw a playground coming up and Jack went around it. Thomas ducked under the monkey bars and high-stepped over the dangling swing, making up precious amounts of time.

One step took them both over the small pond in the park. Turning immediately left, they dodged between two houses and entered the town square. Thomas had almost caught up to Jack when they both leapt from the ground. Thomas hit the courthouse with his hands touching the roof, hanging from his armpits with feet dangling over the abyss below. Jack, suddenly lagging by less than half a second, landed on the roof with both feet.

Jack raised both his hands above his head,

proclaiming, "Victory is mine." Thomas pulled himself over the ledge and sulked quietly. He never won their races. Time and time again, Jack seemed to squeak out the victories. It had crossed Thomas's mind that Jack might be holding back and letting him keep up, but he did not really want to know if it were true.

The two friends lay down, looking up at the stars in the sky with the occasional crow flying past their field of vision. It was a new moon, so they were not pulling large amounts of energy from the Earth's satellite. The night sky looked amazing; their night vision was unparalleled on a normal night, but without the moon to focus on, they could see for light-years into the sky.

They stared out into the infinite space, seeing stars that no human would ever see, small remnants of light reaching the Earth after thousands of years of burning, leaving such a small trace of visibility only the undead would catch the glimpse. The constellations were completely obscured since there were too many stars to see the configurations.

Jack sat up to look out at the city in its familiar scene. Thousands of streetlights, store lights, houselights, headlights… Another view that no one would see unless they took the trek up on top of the courthouse, which no one did. It was just another example of how the world opened to them and them alone, just like the stars, just like people's auras, and just like the sounds of the night.

Beyond the lights of the city were hills and the lake

where Jack had disposed of one of Thomas's victims. Thomas sat up to look at the city. Peering out into the vast world, he felt a warm breeze sweep across him, relaxing his body and allowing him rest.

Thomas allowed the thoughts of Lilith to roam through his mind. "Do you ever associate with humans?" Thomas asked.

Jack smirked, thinking he knew where the conversation was headed. "I don't, other than feeding." Jack smiled, showing his full set of menacing razor-sharp teeth as Thomas looked over, chuckling at the image. "It is not forbidden, if that is what you mean."

"No, that didn't even cross my mind." Thomas searched for the words that kept him from sounding like a prepubescent schoolboy. "I met someone."

Jack got on his hands and knees and slowly crept toward Thomas. The conversation was heading exactly where he expected. "You met someone? You are planning on having relations with a human?" Jack tried to keep the amusement to himself, but it did not work. He let out little bursts of laughter that sent spittle everywhere as his lips were not sealed as tightly as he hoped.

Thomas responded in defense. "No, it's not like that. It isn't exactly sexual. She is just an interesting person."

"You haven't been with a woman in how long and you don't find her attractive?" Jack had crawled over on his fists, his face now in the personal space of Thomas's.

"No, I think she is hot…" Thomas was cut off by

hysterical laughter from Jack. "What the hell?"

Jack broke through his laughter to explain himself to Thomas. "I was just giving you a hard time. As vampires, we don't have a never-ending sex drive." He bowed his head to collect his composure. "But, if one activates it, people better watch out."

"But I thought we were supposed to be extremely sensual beings?" Thomas blurted, thinking of old vampire movies he had seen.

"Almost all of the vampire folklore is based on a few radical vampires. One vampire is born with a sex drive and abuses his ability to understand people and all are labeled sexual deviants. One vampire is allergic to garlic and everyone thinks it will kill all of us. We stay in the shadows so much that every time one of us comes out and causes a scene, the humans create these biological rules that just aren't true.

"There is a book out there somewhere called Known Vampiric Biology that was written by a vampire who was a doctor in his past life. It is a biological explanation of our species. It is hard to track down as it gets passed from vampire to vampire, but it answers all questions."

Jack's tone was one of annoyance. There was little he disliked about the human populace, but mass idiocy was one of them. "But... I digress. What about this woman?"

Thomas proceeded to spill his guts and confessed a deep love for Lilith, still not understanding the attraction. The stars looked down on the two of them as they dealt with their vampire problems as if they were humans.

Jack eventually stood up to leave and in the process, parted from Thomas with his final remarks. "Look, if you like this woman, that is great, but it won't be like it was before you changed. The physical will be different and the emotional attachment will feel skewed. It will be more of a strange paternal relationship than love. But if you want to deal with the pain, be my guest." And with that, Jack dived headfirst off the courthouse.

Thomas continued to stare out into infinity while he thought about Lilith. He could not imagine how hard her life had been over the last few years, having to deal with the loss of her child. The worst part was the fact that she continued to dwell on it. She refused to move on. Thomas would have cried if his body were capable of such things.

He got to his feet and bounded off the building, then he walked slowly through the town. It was still early in the night and he had a while before he had to hide in the church away from the light of day.

He watched people as they passed him in the street. He looked at their aura and peered into their minds. He felt the emotions swirling in their heads, searching for someone with whom he felt that connection like he felt the first time he saw Lilith. It never happened though. No one seemed to be filled with the same pain, the torment, yet still had the desire to continue, still had the passion for the Lord. He began to think he found the only person in the world who he could truly connect with.

His stroll took him through the business district and

around some neighborhoods. In a more expensive neighborhood, he could sense the people in their houses happy with life. They were thankful for their safety and wished to spend more time with their families. The trees arched overhead, creating a canopy to protect them from the dark night sky. The roads were perfectly smooth and complemented the beautiful construction of the mansions that lined the street.

He kept on walking down past the local college. No one seemed to notice him. He wanted to be alone and wander the shadows without a companion, at least as long as Lilith was not with him. He watched as the college kids jumped from bar to bar, staggering drunk through the streets between ventures. Noise was abundant there as it seemed to help the students express their joy.

Down through a poor neighborhood he witnessed a less fortunate set of people wanting nothing more than happiness and safety, putting themselves to bed. The street's pavement was more worn and not well maintained, but the intentions of the people who lived there were no different than the people of the richer neighborhood.

He ended his trek back at the church, standing atop the manhole cover in the center of the street. He felt a desire to plunge down below the surface to the sewer where he most likely would have ended his night. It was almost as if someone were calling him to descend the ladder, a call from one of his parents or grandparents to return home from a day of playing with the neighborhood children. But the knowledge that

Lilith stayed within the walls of the church overpowered those feelings.

He walked up the path and to the doors of the church. The moment he stepped into the church he could hear his steps again, losing his cover of night. He was no longer hiding in the shadows. He could not hide in the church, could not hide from God.

He pushed open the doors into the main hall and saw Lilith sitting in a front pew, bent over, praying through her tears, fighting the pain that was her life. He sat back in the last pew and bent his neck, allowing his head to dangle in respect of his Lord. He tried to pray. He silently spoke for Lilith and how he wanted her to get past her son. He spoke of how he wanted her to one day see the child again in heaven, but until that moment occurred, he wished for nothing more than her ability to be happy once more. He asked for the chance to help bring her to this place of happiness and even if by some unheard miracle, maybe she could feel for him what he felt for her. He ended his prayer with an "amen," although he felt as though he were speaking to himself, unheard by the Creator, but he did it nevertheless.

Soon, he rose from his pew, bowed his head in remembrance of Christ and began walking to the front of the room. When he came in close to Lilith, she turned, startled, to see him approaching her. Then she smiled through her tears and scooted to the side to give him room to accompany her.

Jack's Diary

Could there possibly be redemption?

Jack Year 1611 Day 102 AV

Jack sat beneath the surface of the city, pondering the dilemma that Thomas had let himself fall into. It was a piece of life that Jack missed, but it was so long ago that it felt like a different world, a different life, or a different reality. Sitting in the sludge of the sewers, he considered how his life might have turned out had he not taken that fateful early morning walk. Maybe he would have eventually found love, success, maybe even happiness. But they were all lost possibilities, forever gone.

He tried to suppress his thoughts about Thomas's mission, but he could not thwart the ideas from walking around his head. He wanted so desperately to follow Thomas and have a soul and spread holiness, but the other vision of the world made so much more sense. The idea that he was a child of God was too unbelievable.

He sat back in the sludge and let his dreams and aspirations die under the weight of logic and tradition.

Jack's Diary

Could there possibly be redemption?

Timeus Year 78 Day 187 AB

The loneliness of the rectory crowded Timeus as he let idle thoughts take over his constantly working brain. Ever since Thomas had shown up, he was haunted by the old memories of his redheaded friend, a death that lay squarely on the priest's shoulders. So many years later he wanted to move on, to accept people rather than fear them. He thought it would mean the world if he could allow Thomas to be welcomed into his heart without fear, but the thought died under the weight of his unchanging self and lingering fear. Theories of how to rid the church of Thomas took over.

Jack's Diary

Could there possibly be redemption?

Lilith Year 0 Day 98 BV

She would have thought about the possibilities of her future, but the weight of her loss crushed everything.

Jack's Diary

He has gone too far. I do not want to destroy him, but my first allegiance lies with my maker.

Thomas Year 2 Day 123 AV

The dead of night was always the perfect time to watch people who think they are completely alone. As an old man made the trek that was a nightly ritual for him, Thomas stared down at his aura. The essence of his life packed into a colorful energy that churned with the night air and left an everlasting imprint on their dimension. Thomas could feel the man's grumblings as they echoed throughout his psyche, obviously unhappy with his place in the universe.

As he passed by, the blue vaporish aura was constantly overshadowed by a red tint. Thomas watched as the two colors played with each other, rather than mixing to create a new hue. The man slowly walked down the sidewalk and Thomas looked back the other way, past the crows pecking the ground to wait for the next person.

Suddenly, the bench lurched backward, nearly splintering the wood into Thomas's legs. He looked to his side to see Jack acting nonchalant. The two remained on the bench, watching people walk by and experiencing their view of the world. Eventually, Jack turned to Thomas, determined to speak to him about something.

"I heard you've been feeding a lot." There was no obscurity to his message; it was quite forthright.

"Did I end up in the papers?" Thomas put up his hands as he made a spooky sound. He had decided that there was no use in following Jack's advice. He had been doing whatever he wanted for months now and he had not seen a vampire community ready to chastise him for it. He was not convinced that there was a vampire community.

"Yes. And you shouldn't be so cynical about the consequences of your actions." Jack was aggravated with Thomas's foolish ideas that called to his dreams of acceptance.

"I don't think I believe there are any consequences. And if there are, God is obviously protecting me from them because I haven't seen a single soul…" He paused at the word. "Or nonsoul, as you believe it to be, that cares what I am doing."

"There you go with your 'God' again." Jack utilized his air quotes. But as he put his hands back to his side, he noticed a piece of paper sticking out of Thomas's back pocket. He snatched the paper with his stealthy vampire abilities without Thomas noticing.

Thomas looked at the ground of the sidewalk, watching a couple of ants wander aimlessly around the pavement. They appeared to have no direction, left to wander until the Lord took them home.

Jack did not want to bring attention to the fact that he stole the note from Thomas and read it in silence while Thomas was fixated on the ground.

Society has lost its morals.

"Thou shall not steal." It is one of the oldest laws known to man.

This man disobeyed that decree from Yahweh and he has now suffered his wrath. Take this forward and let it be known that if any man wants to live in God's world, then he must obey his commandments. No man shall dishonor the Creator without feeling the vengeance of his angel.

Sincerely,

The Angel of Yahweh (aka The Embalming Killer)

Jack was stunned. It was obviously directed toward the police to give motive for his crimes. He looked over at Thomas, who was still staring at the pavement. He raised his fist and slammed it into Thomas's face, sending the young vampire flying off the bench and fifty feet down the pavement. Thomas slid on the side of his face, which would have shredded the skin of a normal man, but he reached his feet with no wound to show.

Jack screamed at Thomas, "You couldn't keep it to yourself? You have to be in the spotlight! I asked you to keep out of the papers and now you do this? Forget the papers. People write books and make movies on serial killers who leave motive behind." Jack thought about running over to punch Thomas again, but it would not help except to relieve some of his own stress. He gathered his composure and asked a simple question. "Have you already left one of these with a body?"

Thomas, now standing back in apprehension of another violent outburst, tried to gradually divulge his recent actions. "I have left a few notes in the last few days." Thomas was at a loss of words as he watched Jack's eyes scamper around, looking for peace. "It's why I've been feeding so much recently. I'm on a mission, and I'm trying to make examples of people, but when no one understands the example, then they think you are just some sick murderer. They must understand why I am here and why this is happening. There isn't a person out there…"

Jack cut him off. "It's as if you think you are doing these things for some reason other than you physically have to. It's your biology! This whole mission you have created is in your head. You are delusional. The holy quest you think you're on is nothing more than a way to make you feel better, as if you are not killing the innocent, but smiting the wicked." Jack looked to the ground and muttered to himself, "I can't keep this from him."

Thomas, hearing the utterance, was suddenly alerted to the idea that there may be someone or a group of some ones who could take offense to his own actions. "Who?"

Thomas let it slip, even though he was not going to question Jack when he was so upset. He did not get an answer, just a quizzical look back in his direction. Already committed to the query, he asked more clearly, "Who can you not keep this from?"

Jack shook his head, knowing that he would not tell Thomas unless he had to. "You shouldn't concern yourself with it now. Just stop your crusade. If you want safety, leave religion out of this." That was all Jack said to Thomas. He immediately leapt across the street and disappeared into a gathering of trees.

For the first time, Thomas felt as if he saw Jack's aura as he disappeared with a lingering black wind. Moments after he was gone, the black particles seemed to dance about and taunt Thomas as he stood alone on the sidewalk. Maybe it was aura, or maybe it was his soul, left black from the years of feeling abandoned in the world.

Thomas returned to his bench. Looking up at the cloudy night sky, no stars, no moon, just darkness, he pondered who Jack could be talking about. Jack seemed to have come to terms with the fact that Thomas would not hide in the shadows, but the constant references to God upset Jack because of the mysterious "him." Who would be offended by Christianity? He obviously had to feed, but why did religion change it?

Still staring out into the void of the overcast night, Thomas felt as if the dark clouds fell down upon him. The old, familiar fear of claustrophobia kicked in as he felt an evil in the cloud that could not be described.

Thomas stood up and kicked a rock into the street. He watched it bounce across the asphalt in what seemed to be a random pattern, dodging left, then turning right… But he knew that it was not random. It was the way the asphalt was laid, combined with how he kicked the stone. Reflecting on the rock, he thought maybe his situation was not as random as it felt at that moment.

Thomas knew he was representing good by doing God's work, but maybe Jack was representing evil. Maybe he was doing the work of Satan and trying to pull Thomas in with him. Or maybe they both were and Thomas just did not know it.

Could it be possible that as a vampire he was saved by evil and he was here to do the work of demons? He shook his head, trying to drive the idea out. He could not consider such horrendous ideas. He was there to follow the holy law and that was that.

He knew it was getting to be later in the morning. Three hours until sunup. Rising to his feet, he realized that he had a date with Lilith at the coffeehouse. He called it a date, but it was more of two friends meeting for coffee. She had recently started to get up earlier to spend some time with him since he was never out and about during the day.

Thomas strolled down the street, heading toward the coffeehouse. It was a short distance from the church, a perfect place for them to meet so Thomas could spend the least amount of time getting back before the sun came up over the horizon. For once, he wanted to stay out of the shadows, to be in plain sight while he made his way toward his "neighborhood."

Every streetlight he passed under he felt the energy radiate out from the bulb and tried to steal as much for himself as possible, but it was not like the moon. He could not receive the same sustenance from them. He strained to remember walking in the sun. It was never an activity that he enjoyed, but still a faint memory he wished he could recall. Was strolling under the streetlights anything like walking in the sunlight? Trying to bring a smile to his face, his brain conceded the idea that he would never walk in the sun again, at least without the torturous drain that it caused him.

Thomas turned a corner and the church came into view. His route took him past the church and over the manhole where he thought he began to hear screams of pain bouncing around his brain. A thick fog of pain, torture, and hatred emerged from his own set of thoughts.

Thomas let out a grunt, pulling his mind away from the odd screams and returned to his path to reach Lilith. Down the street and around two more corners he could see the small building snuggled in a strip of pawnshops and antique stores. The construction of the building was one long strip with each business divided by interior walls along with its own awning and sign. The coffee shop had the same red brick walls and two large front windows that all the stores had. The only distinguishing characteristic was its green sign over the windowed door that read, "The Morning Grind."

The door pulled outward and revealed a small, cozy place decorated with the typical wooden tables with high-backed chairs. The occasional couch sat against the wall next to a stack of unused board games. Only a couple of patrons were using the furniture. Wednesday morning was the scene for people grabbing a cup of joe to go in preparation for their morning commute, not for the typical loafer who took up the furniture in the store. Thomas was running through what he wanted to tell Lilith, still attempting to bring her out of the depths of depression.

She had not yet arrived, so Thomas sat down at one of the tables and watched as the two customers sipped their coffee with perfect posture and heads held upward. Both customers were men wearing sandals and pseudo business casual attire made of something that was obviously "Earth friendly," possibly hemp. One had long hair pulled back into a low ponytail and the other had tousled hair just over his ears. He assumed them both to be professors at the college because he hoped it was the only place a person like that would be taken seriously. The coffeehouse was not his scene, but at five a.m., there were few places to go to talk.

Lilith stood in line to get Thomas's and her coffees. Neither of them had much money, but the priest had recently been paying them small sums to clean up the church, doing odd jobs and such. Thomas sat back in his high-backed chair and watched Lilith's body language. She still stood hunched over, staring at the floor. Her long dress, swaying ever so slightly when she would move closer to the front of the line, hung on her like she was a coat hanger.

Thomas felt she did not fit in with the rest of the caffeine-craving customers. She had an air about her that gently whispered reality, while everyone else oozed arrogance and the worst of them gushed with a snootiness that should be beholden by royalty.

It was not often that Thomas saw her outside the church where he could use all of his vampiric senses. Her aura spread wider than most, a perfect magenta that pulsed and stretched far past her skin. Even if he did not have the strange crush on her that he did, her pinkish-purple aura would have caught his eye.

She did not spend much time at the front of the line. She ordered her café mocha and Thomas's carmel latte. After a brief wait at the counter, the barista handed over the drinks and she was on her way over to the table that Thomas had been occupying.

The majority of the morning was spent in awkward silence, with Thomas tapping his fingernails on the side of his steaming hot cup of coffee. Lilith sat across the table from him, slowly sipping her own cup, looking at the floor as usual. Thomas wondered if it were a nervous habit of hers, or if her focus on the ground was another side effect of losing a child. He wished he could understand her nuances and her actions, but there was too much complication to be sure of what caused these things.

Eventually conversation was birthed and they cautiously approached the subjects that bothered each of them. Thomas divulged his own issues. He spoke of being misunderstood and how there may a entire group of people that could be plotting against him. He discussed his dedication to God and how it seemed to be driving a wedge into one of his friendships. He wanted to cryptically talk to Lilith about herself, but after hearing himself talk about his issues, he was afraid he was coming off as somewhat insane.

After Thomas let out his troubles, Lilith took her turn. The topics were the same as usual: her son Amon, her desire to see him again, and her dedication to Father Timeus for helping her.

In the midst of their conversation, the tone moved from a friendly curiosity to pleas for change. "I know that I have no right to tell you how you should live, but I can't stand by and watch you destroy yourself. Life is the most precious gift we have and you need to grab a hold of it. You need to move on." Thomas's voice had moved to a near whining tone in desperation to help his friend.

These conversations had not yet done any good that Thomas could see, but he felt that if he kept praying and talking, then maybe she would turn her life around. Lilith looked up from the ground and into Thomas's eyes. The uncharacteristic move took Thomas aback, but he returned her stare, unmoving from his position. The determination that bled through her soul almost overpowered Thomas as he waited for a response.

"Do you really think that I haven't tried to move on? I have advanced in leaps and bounds." Lilith's knuckles whitened from the intensity she utilized for grasping her cup. "I talk with Father Timeus all the time. I have spoken to you multiple times. I am even out of the church right now. These are huge steps for me. But what of it? I still have nothing. My life hasn't changed. I am still a homeless former mother who has nothing to live for." Her gaze retreated to the safety of the floor. "I used to see beauty all around me, but it all died with him."

Thomas took her hand as gently as possible. He got to his feet and put his coffee cup on the table. Then he led her out the door of The Daily Grind and down the street. The sky was still washed with the black of night, but he knew he did not have ample amounts of time. The sun would rise and he would be stuck wherever he was at the time. His brisk walk forced Lilith to jog behind him. Her arm was outstretched in front of her while she forced her feet to keep moving just to stay up with Thomas.

They quickly reached the library. He pressed a finger to her lips to make sure she would not try to speak to him. It was an unnecessary move since she was dumbfounded about his plans and had no intention of using her vocal chords. He disappeared behind the building, leaving her to wonder what he had in mind, but it was not long before he slid open a window in the front of the building and held out his hands to pull her inside the library.

The inside of a library at night is a relaxing

environment. The lights from the street seep in through the windows that populate the outer walls. Not a single movement exists inside as the books fill the open room as a cemetery is filled with graves. The comparison sat well with Lilith, walking down man-made aisles, looking to either side, seeing the proof that a life at least once existed. It was humbling as well as peaceful.

Thomas held her hand and led her through a maze of shelves as he dodged the security cameras. There was not much challenge in hiding from the security as the tall shelving units provided abundant cover from their view. The cool air brushed past Lilith's face as they took a turn toward the back of the building. The scent of old paper was unmistakable, reminding them both of where they were.

Thomas barreled through a door and started ascending the stairs faster than Lilith thought possible. Her inability to keep up caused him to turn around and lift her into his arms. Then he bounded up the stairs and Lilith stared into the colorless eyes of her friend. She could not help but think of her youth and how her father would carry her different places without any expectations from her, only seeking her happiness. She noticed a strange similarity in her relationship with her father and her relationship with Thomas.

After four flights of stairs, Thomas kicked open a thick, steel door to unveil the magnificence of their town from the roof of the building. The scene still brought a smile to his face, regardless of how many times he had seen it.

Going through the peacefulness of the library before viewing the city from the roof was an added experience that outshined normalcy, where he would just leap up the side of the building.

Lilith was in awe. Her mouth gaped open, her eyes nearly popping out from between their lids. The sight was unrivaled to anything she had seen before. The sky was still darkened although the sun was threatening to rise. Down on the street, the citizens were beginning their day. Cars began to fill the streets and the early risers were out with their children and their pets getting a little fresh air to start the morning.

Thomas grabbed Lilith hard by both shoulders and looked deep into her eyes. He bared his own soul to her without saying a word. The intensity of the hold sent reverberations throughout her body, a chill that she did not want to leave. Suddenly, the sight from the roof was overshadowed by the passionate stare that the vampire was burning into her existence.

"This is beauty." Thomas broke the silence with a tone that screamed passion. "If there is no other reason to live, it is this: the people, the patronage, the nature, the sheer fact that the world has come this far. Don't you want to be a part of this?" It no longer mattered what Thomas had to say. Lilith was captive to his words. She wanted nothing but that moment for the rest of eternity.

Thomas wanted to continue in a dramatic monologue. He wanted to tell her that it did not matter what had been or what would be. The now was what mattered. The beauty of the world required everyone to be a part of it and without her, it would not be the same place. He wanted to know if she had passed on and her son was still there, what would she want him to do, but it did not matter.

She leaned in and kissed him, breaking his stare and forcing him to experience emotions that should have stayed foreign to his vampiric self. Her lack of knowledge of the undead and his specific situation may have changed her thoughts, but it was inconsequential after the kiss. Their lips held together for much longer than was safe for Thomas. They held the lock until the sun began to change the color of the sky. Still, no sunbeams coming over to threaten Thomas's physical well-being, he pulled away from her. He did not speak to her, but it was unnecessary. The moment they had shared spoke to both of them from deep within.

She closed her eyes as Thomas picked her up in his arms. He leapt off the building without her knowing and slid down a drainpipe. She just snuggled her head into his chest with the first true smile erupting from her face in years. The walk back to the church with his love in his arms was something that Thomas had wanted to experience in his first life but never had the chance. All of his misunderstood feelings for Lilith sank away, leaving a puddle of new emotions, ones of love, ones of infatuation. There was no longer anything he wanted except to be with her.

Thomas stood in front of the church holding Lilith in his arms. Her bony shoulder wedged into his upper chest, creating what would normally have been a sharp pain, but he did not notice with his lack of nerves. Her other arm was up across his chest with her hand laid gently behind his neck. He stepped up to the door of the church, pushing the large oak gate open with his hip. Then he carried his new love across the threshold of their current home, what felt a fitting end to their surprising and sudden love affair.

He set her down on one of the last pews next to Father Timeus. She wanted him to stay, she wanted him to spend the rest of the day with her, but she knew that her abrupt happiness should be given a chance to blossom on its own. Thomas walked through the church hall toward the staircase, the first light of the morning now visible through the windows of the building. He was sorry he put her down. He wanted to stay. Then he told himself that it was what she needed. She could use a pep talk from the priest and he had the rest of her life to spend time with her.

He took the lonely walk down the spiral stairs, allowing his echoing footsteps to ping a new thought in his head with each step. Thud, a step shot images of Lilith standing beside him. Thunk, a second step he realized that he would eventually be alone again. Boom, his next step echoed and he realized he had not been truthful with Lilith. He stopped before he reached the bottom of the stairs, pondering the possibility of telling Lilith about his vampirism. Was his relationship too new for that kind of revelation? Would she still care for him or would she feel he was not human? The questions piled up in his head as he hopped to the bottom of the stairs. Silently, he lay down on his cot with the light turned out. The blackness seemed to speak to him. She will know soon enough.

Thomas did not know how to interpret the fictitious voice in his head, but he assumed that he would work it out soon. She needed a few hours to herself and he would see her in the evening.

Letter to the Pope

With no word from the Vatican, I will remove the demons myself.

Timeus Year 78 Day 284 AB

He shook his head in fictitious disapproval as he led Lilith out the door of the church. She was happy for once and he knew that his little stunt would only serve to injure that mood.

The priest knew that she needed the money and he promised to pay her for her work, but it was the only way to rid the sanctuary of Thomas. He may have provoked her to take the money, he may have suggested that he did not mind, but it was all the excuse he needed to send her away.

He knew that Thomas would not stand for her being gone and he may fight it, but he also knew he would not leave her alone on the streets. All Timeus could hope for was that they would find somewhere else to haunt.

He ignored his conscience, the voice of God in many cases. Instead, he rejoiced in the idea that in a few hours Thomas would be gone forever.

Known Vampiric Biology

The powers of a vampire are somewhat mystical, but emotion is known to play a role in their magnitude.

Thomas Year 2 Day 123 AV

Thomas had spent nearly an hour lying on his cot and wondering if the sun had gone down. No sleep, of course. He had not slept in a couple of years. He had spent the entire day staring into darkness and thinking about his moment with Lilith. The kiss they shared that morning would be burned into his mind for infinite amount of time. It took all of his will to stay in the basement while she had time to herself.

Excited to talk to her about their situation, he jumped up from his cot, stumbling in the dark in an attempt to make his way to the stairs in record time. Each step he took could not come fast enough as he rose from the depths of the church. Pushing open the door, the first things that came into his vision were the candles lit on the chandeliers. His mind darted back and forth, realizing that the sun had receded and the night now belonged to Lilith and him. He searched the room over with his white eyes but saw nothing except for Father Timeus standing in front of the darkened Pearly

Gates-stained glass.

A look of dread came across the priest's face as he quickly made his way over to Thomas. Knowing something unpleasant was coming made the moment surreal for Thomas, causing the room to feel as if it were tilting back and forth. It was such a frightening instant that his equilibrium barely withstood the horror.

Timeus came over to him with such grace he seemed as though he were hovering over the floor. "Thomas, I want to tell you that I am sorry." Father Timeus refused to look into the terrifying eyes of the vampire, hoping that Thomas would not realize what had actually happened.

"There was a situation this afternoon. Lilith came to me and told me of your actions this morning. She spoke of love and marriage and I was overjoyed for both of you. It seemed as though God had taken you by the hand to lead you both out of the pit you have been wallowing in."

Thomas listened closely, but he could not concentrate on the words. There was something bad coming and his mind rejected all information that was unrelated. "What is wrong?" he replied, as if the priest were dancing around the important matters.

The priest was engulfed by his terror of the man whom he knew must be an evil entity. "There are rules that must be followed around here. And although we are a recognized homeless shelter, I can not allow someone to stay here if they break certain rules." The priest fell into the role of a shy preteen, sweeping his foot across the floor while he stared down at it. He fumbled his hands behind his back, trying to decide if Thomas was going to get violent.

Losing his patience, Thomas's words were now more direct. "What do you want to tell me?" There was a growl in his voice that was unintentional. He could not disguise his fears or annoyances anymore.

Timeus's breaths became shorter and more consistent. "I had to ask Lilith to leave today." The words came out in a quick succession, as if it were a Band-Aid being ripped off. The priest watched Thomas as his eyes narrowed and his jaw clenched. Timeus's vocal pace went from fast to frantic in flat-out fear. "She is welcome to mass. All of God's children are welcome to mass, but"

Thomas cut off the priest. "What did she do?" He tried to soften his voice, but the commanding spirit of his personality forced through.

"I caught her taking money from the collection." He did not continue. The revelation was final in his mind. Anything more and he might give away too much.

"Are you sure it was her? Did you ask her why? I can't believe she would do that." Thomas was in a state of confusion. He did not want his new love to be banned from his only safe haven.

"I saw her myself." Timeus bowed his head in respect to Thomas. "I was very upset at the time and she was crying. I am not sure what she said, but it is something that can not be tolerated. I am sorry. But when she left, there was a man with her. He said he knew you and would take care of her until you got up. A tall, pale man. I think his name was Jack."

Jack's name alarmed Thomas although there was no reason for it. There was something amiss about the whole situation with Jack never wanting to be near the church. He felt there were not good intentions in his motives. His skin seemed to tighten and his teeth felt a tingle run through each of them. Now, that vampire who wanted him to stop spreading the Word of God was with his love, whether it was for good or evil, and the woman he would kill for had committed the sin that he vowed to eradicate.

Father Timeus saw an unease fill Thomas's eyes and he desperately wanted the unholy being out of his church. "I am sorry, Thomas. I know the two of you were getting close."

Thomas was not listening to the priest. His mind was awash with worry about his love. Where had she gone? He quickly switched to pleading with Father Timeus before he gave into his mind and went out searching for Lilith.

"There is another side to the story. I know it. She needs to stay here, or she will revert back to her pain. It took me months to get her to open up. Please, Father."

The man of God had a fiery desire to rid his church of the vampire, and although he may be giving him an opening to return, he would have said anything at that point to get him out.

"She is better than that. When I find her, if I bring her back, will you hear her out?" Thomas was letting the words just pour out of his mouth, no thought, just unregulated blubbering.

"I may have been too hasty. Please do bring her back so we can discuss these things." Timeus immediately turned away to make his way back to his office, annoyed with his morality butting in and creating another possible visit from the vampire.

Thomas was relieved that she was being given some grace. But he had no time to lose. He needed to find Lilith before she fell back into depression. All he had to do was find Jack. He tried to keep his mind away from the disturbing possibilities of Jack's motives.

He ran as fast as he could to the front door. It was only slightly faster than he could before he turned into a vampire, but he felt as though he were moving in slow motion. The floors creaked as normal with each step Thomas pushed down. The walls left him feeling like he was being watched as he tried to force time to move faster as he made his way through the first set of doors and then toward the large oak entrance.

He pushed the huge oak door open, leaving himself out in the real world. His vision and hearing returned to their super-intensified state as he looked to either side, trying to envision where Lilith would have run off to.

The quiet sound of paper rustling in the wind caught Thomas's attention. He turned around to see a note wrapped around the iron handle of the church door. Subconsciously, he knew that the note was for him, but his body resisted the instinct to read it. He swallowed hard as he forced his legs to approach the paper.

Unraveling it from the handle, he noticed the red ink was still wet on the paper, admitting that the person who left it was just there.

I had to take her. I told you to stop your relentless prattle about God's work. Now there is no remorse for your actions and you must pay the price. I am sorry for your loss, but you must learn to respect the clan. If you stop spreading the lies about your so-called savior, then Lilith will be returned. Otherwise, we will soon come for your head.

You've been warned,
Jack

Letter to God

I may have made a mistake.

Timeus Year 78 Day 284 AB

Timeus heard a deep scream of sorrow come from outside the church and he instinctively knew that something had happened to Lilith. His actions may have caused another innocent life to be taken for no reason other than his own fears.

Visions of the redheaded boy flashed in his mind and he understood that this was a second chance which he destroyed. Decades after his first unintentional murder, he struck again, leaving him with a crippled hope that he may be given one last chance at forgiveness.

Only then did regret set in.

Known Vampiric Biology

Force is not an issue of a vampire. Without the ability to feel pain, their muscles can deliver far beyond that of a normal man.

Thomas Year 2 Day 124 AV

The note lay motionless in Thomas's hands with the ink finally drying into stains on the parchment, quickly transforming Thomas into a being of rage. His mind had convinced him that the worst had already happened to Lilith and there was no way left to save her. He hated Jack. Whether there was a clan of vampires behind him or not, Thomas would find him and end his existence.

It was so clear. Jack figured out what would get to Thomas and he acted on it, but why? His mind buzzed from one thought to the next without any cohesiveness. Vengeance. Death. Loss. There was no rhyme or reason to his thought patterns.

The image of Lilith dead in the street kept creeping into his mind, the thought intensifying his rage and leaving him wanting revenge. He was not going to turn over and just take it. Scanning every conversation he ever had with Jack, the only thing that stuck out in his mind was his hatred of

God. If he wanted a fight, then Thomas could show up to the game.

If Jack thought Thomas had been spreading the Word of God before, he had no idea what was coming. Thomas looked to the heavens, seeing nothing but the moon and a few stars through the cloudy sky. He gave a smile to God as he formulated his plan to let the world know what he had been doing.

Then Thomas turned and began running down the street almost instantly, building speed to be moving quickly and bounding down the road, running between cars, passing them as he increased his momentum. His steps pounded the ground, causing cracks in the pavement, showing his disregard for anything but his own agenda. Paying no attention to his appearance, he refused to move stealthily, causing panic in the streets as he smashed into the sides of cars that got in his way.

Citizens pulled over in awe of the speeding man, calling the police and reporters about the situation.

Thomas flew through the city, trying to find the most visible place for his message when he realized it would be the courthouse. Hoping to attract a slew of reporters, Thomas crashed into buildings, destroyed cars and knocked over fire hydrants on his way to the square.

There were flashing blue and red lights chasing him before he got to where he was going. The sirens chased him down roads. Occasionally, one would appear in his pathway trying to cut him off, but he just leapt over them and cackled as he passed.

His anger continued to intensify as he neared the courthouse. His vampiric powers even seemed to be directing the weather as dark clouds rolled in over the town, causing random lightning strikes around his target building. The only beings that felt safe within the storm were the crows that infested the city.

A single jump put Thomas on top of the courthouse, looking down on the cops who trailed him to his destination. A strong vibration rang throughout his hands and his vision was covered in a translucent red, coinciding with the fury he had built up that manifested in such a way he was almost levitating above the rounded roof of the courthouse.

He looked down upon the gathering crowd and noticed a couple of news cameras pointing in his direction, alerting him that this was the time to announce his mission. He took a deep breath and envisioned what would follow.

He could see the pitchforks and torches marching down the streets in search of vampires. A vision of police and military arming themselves to fight the undead flashed before his eyes. If Jack was worried about past witch hunts, he had a rude awakening coming his way.

When Thomas began to speak, his voice rumbled with such force that the windows of the nearby stores rattled. "Those of you who have been following me know me as the Embalming Killer." The clouds above Thomas began to swirl very slowly as if a weakened tornado were forming over his head. "You have mislabeled me! I am an angel of God. I am the messenger of our savior. I am the enforcer of the Eighth Commandment."

Lightning struck the ground around the police who were trying to organize in order to start shouting at Thomas through their bullhorns. Rain poured from the sky, soaking Thomas as he rose completely off his feet and hovered twenty feet above the courthouse.

"There is no need to fear me unless you are a sinner, a putrid dreg of a society that has forgotten how to worship your Creator. My message has been silenced until now. The world must understand my holy quest."

Windows around the square began to crack from the intensity of his voice. The people on the ground threw their hands over their ears to protect themselves from the ever-increasing decibels.

"I am not a normal human." Thomas was about to speak of his change to the undead when he noticed Jack standing on a roof across the street from where Thomas floated. Under his arm hung a struggling Lilith. Her thin bones seemed to be bending unnaturally, her hair twisting in the wind, and she was screaming through a barrage of rain pounding her face.

Thomas fell back to the roof of the courthouse and without saying a word, he hurdled toward Lilith chasing Jack. Jack was running ahead of Thomas by nearly a quarter mile, but Thomas was catching up quickly.

Afraid that Thomas would catch him, Jack jumped off the roofs and down to the street, moving at unimaginable speeds. Thomas followed suit and flew off of a building toward the street. As Jack made impact with the street, sending a shockwave of cracks down the road, Lilith fell limp. Her body dangled in the torrential downpour.

Thomas, fearing that Lilith could not survive the impact of the fall, increased his speed, moving so quickly his eyes almost could not stay open. Jack realized that he could not outrun Thomas anymore and started to tear down fixtures to create obstacles for his pursuer.

A streetlight came crashing down into the road, causing an explosion of sparks as it smashed into the flooded street. Thomas easily hopped over the blasting electronics, still increasing his speed. The storm cloud now turned a fiery red, twisting and churning, creating forceful winds that were whipping the water up out of the street. It followed Thomas as he hunted Jack. Unbeknownst to him, it was fueled by his rage and reacted to his vampiric senses.

A fire hydrant was thrown at Thomas's head, but a quick dodge avoided it. A car was overturned, but proved to not be a problem for Thomas. Each step he took he came closer to Jack. Inching toward his prey, he could see Lilith swaying in the wind, her head bouncing from side to side depending on Jack's momentum. Her arm was twisted with the elbow bending the wrong direction, a bone broken from the debris that Jack had plowed through.

Thomas screamed out in his booming voice, "You better not let me catch you!" Windows nearby shattered, car alarms sang out loud from the vibrations. The rain had become so horrendous that the sewers were flooding, trash and rodents flowed through the streets after being flushed out of the gutters.

Jack, knowing that he was going to be caught and possibly beheaded, stopped in midstride, leaving Lilith with a whiplash effect. Thomas passed Jack before he noticed he had ceased movement and abruptly turned back to catch him, just in time to receive a manhole cover to the face. Thomas fell back in the center of the road with his skull cracked open, his blood mixing with the waters streaming down the road which nearly covered his face. A streak of dark purple blood washed down the avenue, leaving a trail of metaphorical breadcrumbs to Thomas's head.

Jack continued down the road as Thomas sat up, shaking the throbbing from his face. His wound had already begun healing when he returned to his chase. Jack cut a corner too close and smashed through the edge of a cinderblock wall. Lilith took the brunt of the hit, breaking one of her legs and causing some internal injuries.

Thomas was moving much faster than Jack and was almost within an arm's reach of Lilith. Moving nearly a hundred miles per hour, he saw her head bobbing up and down, blood now pouring out of her mouth. Her arm was mangled and barely held on by the skin. Her leg was not in much better shape. Just before Thomas reached out to grab her, Jack dove into a gutter on the side of the road, splashing into the water before he entered the sewer.

Thomas changed his direction and dove in after them.

With the sewer system completely flooded, they swam through the dark sewage. Jack moved quickly through the water, still holding Lilith under his right arm. Thomas's super sight allowed him to see through the dark murky water. He saw Lilith, awakened by the cold water, her eyes widened in pain as her limbs coiled unnaturally in the water. She gasped for breath, inhaling a lungful of contaminated water and releasing a mouthful of blood that seems to hang motionless in the water until Thomas swam through it.

Sensing her terror, Thomas attempted to reach out to Lilith, but just as he was about to touch her, he was hit in the leg with another manhole cover. His knees dislocated, causing his lower leg to swing sideways while his upper leg remained still. The huge steel disc bounced from his knee to his ankle, crushing it and snapping his tibia.

Thomas let out a deep yowl that somehow echoed throughout the water. He was forced to stop moving to keep his leg from ripping through the skin and severing off forever.

Gingerly, he sat at the bottom of the water on his good knee, afraid that Lilith had drowned or bled to death. He tried to cry, but no tears would come. Looking down to see if his leg was healing, he saw the water receding. Looking up, he realized that he was in the main sewage tunnel just below the entrance to the church. All of the water was gushing to the center of the room.

The final gallons of the sewage flowed into a hole in the center of the floor, where he assumed the manhole cover came from. He remained seated for a couple of minutes while his bones reconnected and his leg returned to normal.

Water continued to drizzle into the room from the storm above which Thomas created, but the room was essentially emptied. For the first time, Thomas could see the passage in the center of the room leading to what appeared to be a dark and hot cavern.

He collected himself and slid down the ladder into the floor to discover a new and terrible place. Upon hitting the ground and turning away from the ladder, Thomas was frozen in time. No matter how much struggle he put up, he could not move.

The room was an apparent abandoned subway tunnel with rails on the floor, a boarding platform in the middle. The exit tunnels had collapsed a long time ago, leaving the room to be sealed from the outside world with the exception of the entry into the sewer. There was an immense heat, blurring all vision into a wave behind the warmth.

He could see Jack out of the corner of his eye kneeling down and looking at the floor. Lilith was suspended in midair, her broken limbs dangling at her sides. She appeared to be unconscious and still bleeding from the mouth. A puddle of her blood had collected on the tiled floor below her at the feet of a tall man. He was very hefty, with scars all over his body in a strange pattern that appeared to be some ancient language. He stood staring at Thomas with skin so pale his internal organs bled through the tint of skin. He wore nothing but a loincloth, standing with a fist on each hip. His smile was terrifying, with his teeth all yellowed and sharpened to a point, just like Thomas's and Jack's.

He laughed as Thomas was dragged to his feet against his will by an invisible force. When the laughter stopped, the only sound that could be heard was the pitter-patter of the rain two levels above.

Absolute terror surged through Thomas's veins. His limbs would not respond to his brain as he attempted to move the tiniest bit. Every time he tried to maneuver his body, he was met with a pressure that forced him into his current stance. Minutes went by with the large man staring and laughing at Thomas's inability to move. His stare bore into Thomas's mental security, convincing him that the man was much more powerful than he.

One more time, Thomas struggled to turn his body, but the moment he tried, his body refused and began to bow down into a kneeling position. His knees smashed into the tile, cracking a couple of the light blue squares. His kneecaps cracked along with the tiles, but he healed almost instantaneously. His head looked up toward the scarred man while his hands rose in front of him. His palms pressed against each other as if he were about to pray. Thomas fought with all his might, but there was no use. He was nothing more than a puppet in that room.

Lilith's mangled and broken body hovered in front of Thomas. He could see the wreckage that Jack had done to her. Her arm was broken in multiple places and had gone completely limp. Both of her legs were broken in at least one place, hanging in a morbid fashion, decorated with dark green bruising all up and down her legs. Blood had dripped out of her mouth and all down her dress, soaking the fabric so her breasts and ribs were outlined perfectly through the blood-drenched material. She had lost most of her color from the severe blood loss but appeared to be breathing. Thomas did not think there was a possibility she could survive.

She hovered around the room a couple of times, spreading the putrid fragrance of her infected wounds until she landed softly on what appeared to be an altar, almost identical to the one Thomas had seen so many times in the church. Upon impact, Lilith did not stir at all, not a sign of consciousness.

The large man rose above the ground and hovered over to Thomas. He looked down into the young vampire's gaze, then grabbed him by the back of his head. His hand remained there with a firm yet calming grasp. The colorless eyes opened wide as the man began to speak.

"I should introduce myself. I am King Eden, the creator of your acquaintance, Jack. I was birthed to the name Cain, son of Adam, from the Garden of Eden." The man tilted his head just a tad. His deep, dignified voice zeroed in on Thomas's attention. "I am the first of your kind, what you call vampires. I am your true creator and you have betrayed me."

Thomas tried to move his mouth, but nothing came out. He could not form words to react to Cain, but his thoughts were sensed by the scarred son of Adam. So you are the one who has been trying to get me to end my crusade against sinners. The thought flew through Thomas's mind and to his surprise, Cain vocalized an answer.

"You have been deluded by my immortal enemy. You believe to be doing a sacred deed when, in fact, you have been shunned by God. Through no fault of your own, God is punishing you. He has banned you from heaven because of my actions thousands of years ago."

Cain turned with his hands behind his back, taking large steps back toward the altar where Lilith was lying. "As a vampire, you have no connection to God. You only exist to defeat him and to reign in his kingdom. God, Yahweh, he is the tormentor; he is the tyrant of our people. He oppresses thousands of my children for no reason, other than they are my children. Sins of the father…"

Thomas felt attacked by Cain's insinuations of the Lord and wanted to retaliate. You did not save me. God saved me. He is the reason I still walk this earth. He is the reason I am not burning in eternal damnation. Thomas was cut off by Cain.

"You don't think this is damnation?" Cain's voice had grown to a roar. The tunnel around them shook from the power of his words. "Welcome to the land of Nod, banished to walk the earth as a night dweller for all of eternity. Until Christ or God himself enter back into your body, you will be forced to continue existing."

Thomas felt there was a disconnect somewhere.

There was an unjustifiable hatred toward the one true Creator. He kept flashing his eyes over toward Lilith, trying to make sure she was still breathing.

Cain noticed the constant attention to the girl, so he hovered over to her. "You want to make sure she's OK? She's alive because I am maintaining her. If it were up to God, she would be dead by now, but I'm merciful enough to not let that life end."

Cain landed on the ground and walked over to Thomas, still kneeling before him. "You don't trust my motives. You don't believe I'm in the right." Cain sat down on the floor in front of Thomas, running his tongue across the tips of his pointed, decaying teeth.

Thomas felt Cain intruding into his mind, pushing out Thomas's thoughts to insert his own. He struggled for a few moments trying to keep sane, but it was no use. Cain was inside his head. Thomas, having no control, felt like he did the first time he fed, nothing more than a spectator in his own body. Then his body rose into the air, outstretching all his limbs to a near-breaking point. His eyes rolled back into his head, and Cain's voice echoed inside his skull.

The Mark

Although he has sinned against me, your retaliation will only harm yourself.

Cain Year 0 Day 0

"I had true life in a time of beauty and perfection. We lived with no disgrace, or at least I thought there was none. The Garden of Eden was a land of exquisite faultlessness, the soil itself was as smooth as clay with the laxity of desert sand. I could cultivate all the food that I knew of. I tended to the land, taking care of produce for the family while my brother Abel tended to the flocks.

"My brother was one of the greatest men to ever grace this earth. He held sympathy for animals that no one has possessed since. He felt their pain and grieved for each one that was led to slaughter.

"The story of my persecution has been twisted by man in an attempt to understand the motives of God. Mortals can not comprehend his vengeance and in their effort to do so, have labeled me a jealous murderer, but it is not true. I still grieve for my brother, who met the sword because of the tormenting master of our universe.

"I still remember that day. The sun stood overhead sending an unrelenting barrage of heat down upon me. I was making the trek from the East River, bringing water to my gardens. It had not rained for weeks and I had to keep the plants alive. I recall wishing I could do what Abel did: watching after his flock at the edge of the West River, dipping his body into the water when the heat became unbearable. But, there was no point in yearning when I had my place in life.

"As I walked back to the garden, my feet calloused beyond repair, covered in the burning soil of Eden. I mused over which of my crops I was to present to the Lord. The season had been harsh on the plants, and the winter would arrive very soon, so I worried about the safety of my family.

"My brother would be strong enough to survive the harsh cold regardless due to his young vitality, but our parents seemed weak. It was just my youth and ignorance; they were stronger than I. Knowing that the crops would cease their production in the coming weeks, I decided to forgo tithing and present the edges of my crops to the Lord. I kept the majority of the plants to assure my family could survive and God would receive the outer ten percent.

"When I reached the garden, I kneeled down in regret that I could not afford to leave the edges and still sacrifice to our Creator, but I knew what I had to do. I reaped what I could give to God and bundled it up in a sacrifice that I took to the circle that evening.

"The circle was a patch of death among Eden. There

was no life within it. It had soil that was dry and hard. No vegetation could survive inside the round, sandy pit. Upon entering the circle there was a sense of destruction. It is the one place on this planet you never want to visit.

"My brother and I reached the circle with our offerings to our Lord. I placed my crops into the circle and watched as they withered and died. The seeds shriveled and browned as the circle took the offering. My brother, Abel, with pain in his face, placed two of the newborns from his flock. He looked away as the animals cried in pain as their bodies caught fire and all their internal moisture dried up. It was not long before there was nothing but dust left in the circle."

Known Vampiric Biology

The origin of vampires is unknown but dates back to the beginning of man.

Cain Year 0 Day 1 AV

"That night was spent sleeping under the stars as usual in Eden. I was next to my brother and both of us were feeling joyous about our dedication to the Lord. I slept that night upon the soft grass with the warmth of Eden caressing my body. It was pure ecstasy, but it would be the last night I would ever spend in the Paradise. The next day would be my entry into hell, my banishment to Nod, and my first day of undeath.

"In the morning, we arose just as the sun came over the horizon. I now wish I would have savored that sunrise, for now, thousands of years later, I can not enjoy them. We each made our way to our workplaces. Abel was overjoyed to see that his flock seemed to have fattened overnight with four of his flock suddenly pregnant. He thanked Yahweh for his good fortune and was happy to see his sacrifice was appreciated.

"I, on the other hand, walked to my garden in

disbelief. Already sweating from the torment of the sun, I approached a barren patch of ground. All of the crops had become infested with insects and nothing was left for sustenance. I fell to my knees in humiliation. Tears fled from my eyes while I pleaded with God to return something so that my family could survive the upcoming cold.

"But it was clear that I was the one who had made the mistake. I had not given to God something of worth. My brother had wept at the death of his flock that he voluntarily gave to the Creator, but I gave to him as a chore, a responsibility instead of out of love. I had not wept for the loss of my crops. Instead, I put them in the circle with no emotion at all. This was the end of the story that the Lord bestowed upon Moses. The rest was man's interpretation of God's actions. But, the rest of the tale in Genesis was inaccurate. My life ended that day.

"Abel came upon my garden later in the afternoon. I was covered in the dust of the earth as I had scavenged the garden in search of just one seed that had survived, but I found nothing. Abel came into the barren land and spoke with compassion for my plight. 'God did not accept your sacrifice? My brother, my poor brother, we can plead to the Lord and he will grant you a second chance. We must find a more deserving tribute to please him.'

"He may not have said it, but it was Abel's idea. I slay my brother in that garden. My bare hands took his life, the hardest thing I ever did. I did not leave that spot until the sun threatened to set. I spent the day tortured in the heat, breathing the dust of the earth lying atop my deceased sibling, weeping over his tragic end.

"As darkness began to overtake the light, I dragged Abel to the circle. Knowing that there was no sacrifice greater than my greatest companion, I tossed his body into the circle and watched as his skin and bones melted into the dryness of death. I looked to the heavens, deep into the stars and for the first time, I heard the voice of God.

"Thunder rumbled from all around; the ground shook, and a deafening voice rattled in my head. 'What have you done? The ground screams to me. Your brother screams to me. The air screams to me. What have you done to your brother?'

"I was lost. My Lord had again not accepted my sacrifice. I tried to plead with him. 'I gave him to you. My last sacrifice was not enough to please you, so I gave you the one thing that I feel I could not live without.' Tears again streaming down my face, I fell to the ground in a fetal position.

"God came thundering back inside my skull, unrelenting and inescapable. 'You have no right. You are not your brother's keeper. You have committed the indefensible. You are banished from the garden and from humankind. Your crops will never bloom. You will be a wanderer forevermore, never receiving the balance of slumber. Food will not resolve your hunger, only the blood in which you spilt will bring any relief.'

"There are no words to describe what I felt. There

was never a moment after that where I felt a love for God. He took my brother from me and then condemned me for it.

"'If that is my punishment, I will be killed by any man who realizes that I offended you,' I said.

"As God spoke to me, a painful searing came across most of my body. 'You will not be vulnerable to death. I give you the mark so that any man who tries to attack you will be warned that vengeance will be fatal.'

"So this is the end of life? I am condemned for eternity?"

"As my child, I can release you from your fate. You must repent for what you did and take me back into your life through my son. There will be a savior and by taking his body into yours and accepting the true light, you will be returned to my kingdom."

"A storm came into Eden with great winds that pushed me out until I was thrown into the mouths of the two rivers. I swam across and upon reaching the bank outside of Eden, the storm subsided. I was left on the outside of Paradise, no chance to say good-bye to my parents, nothing to help me grieve for my brother, just banishment.

"It was there that I wandered, in the land of Nod, scavenging for blood, leaving carcasses to rot. By night I was a predator, but by day, I tried to find shade to keep away the torture of the sun. I was alone for many years until the Great Flood washed Eden away and I was in the company of men again. But even then, I was treated as a leper, with my scars that God imprinted on me. I was tortured during the day and avoided at night. My biology was unnatural.

"I created many vampires before I understood how everything worked, having to drain the body fully to keep them from rising from the dead. Eons of me and my clan trying to fight God, steal as many of his children from him as possible, and force our way back into heaven."

Jack's Diary

I think he understands now.

Lilith Year 0 Day 1 AV

The echoes subsided inside of Thomas's mind. Suddenly, he was free to think on his own again. His body lowered to the ground and the pressure floated away. Left on one knee, he looked up, seeing Lilith lying near death on the altar. He sprang to his feet, running full vampiric speed toward her, but he smashed his body into an invisible wall keeping him from her. Back on the ground, he watched as his knee swelled from the impact and within seconds, reduced its size back to normal.

Thomas turned toward Cain, his anger seething under his ashen skin. He clenched his teeth, the points of his incisors nearly ripping open his gums as his mind raced with ways to dispose of the old vampire when he was suddenly thrown backward. He flew through the air flipping over until he landed headfirst on the abandoned subway track.

Cain stepped forward and spoke so they could all hear. "Stand down. You may have harnessed much energy, but you are no match for my might. Do not worry.

Everything will be fine."

Thomas, frozen in place again, screamed out, trying to tell Cain that if Lilith dies, so will he, but a strange screech is all that left his lips.

Cain smiled as he read Thomas's mind. His tongue slithered in his mouth, visible through the skin of his cheeks. "Your love will be all right. She is only here to get your attention because I cannot have you espousing holy propaganda when you are my son, in a sense. I am the reason all vampires exist and they all honor me for giving them such a gift, while Yahweh is our enemy. He is keeping you from the everlasting kingdom of heaven." Cain's smile turned to a scowl.

Cain let Thomas free again and Thomas charged Cain once more. He was allowed to get closer this time, but was thrown to the ceiling before he reached his target. The back of Thomas's skull slammed into the cavernous roof and was suspended there, no rebound.

Thomas tried to throw his thoughts at Cain. How can you call it propaganda? You are being punished for murdering your brother, for giving God someone else's portion of your crops. If you were repentant, this would all end for you. Thomas was going to continue, but his thoughts were forced out of his head and replaced by the tortured screamings of souls who had been trapped by Cain.

Standing directly below Thomas, Cain stared up at him and in a calm tone replied, "If God is punishing me, why are you being punished? Why are you immortal? Why are you banned from heaven? Why are you left to feed off the blood of the loved? You don't seem to get it. God is controlling and overbearing and evil."

Cain's demeanor went sour again as he raised his voice to ear-shattering levels. "He condemned me for using free will with good intentions! He damned me for honoring him!" Cain looked down at the ground and almost whispered the end of his statement. "The only way out for any of us is to take the hand of Christ and accept it into our bodies, but Christ is gone and he left us with no hope. We are dead to the Lord."

The storm continued to rage up on the surface. The sounds of thunder crept into the cave through the dripping opening in the ceiling. Thomas was released again, falling to the floor, but mercifully, he was slowed before he hit the ground. He knew that there was no chance of attacking Cain. His attempts had failed twice already. He looked to each side. Lilith lay upon the altar with faintest breaths moving her chest up and down. Jack remained in a kneeling position facing Cain.

Thomas tried to think about Lilith, but his thoughts were immediately discarded and replaced by the thunderous voice of Cain. You have not grasped our oppression. He has taken away our right to die! Thomas did not even have a chance to think of a response, for his thoughts were answered by Cain before he formulated them. You think I could end it all with a prayer as though I have the freedom to repent. How do you know I am not forced to have these thoughts? I could be God's puppet, forced to endure so his universe can have a perceived evil presence, just so his supposed goodness can exist. I try every second to fight my persecution, but creatures such as you try to remind the world that we exist, just so God can have his precious little example for all to gawk at.

The words were so invasive, Thomas felt as though he were possessed. He scratched at his ears with a physical attempt to get the thoughts out of his head, but it did nothing except break the skin and leave a momentary stream of his own venom trickling down his face.

Cain walked over to Thomas and placed a hand on his head, his voice unexpectedly soft with compassion. "Calm down. There is no need to fight. I will be a better father than he. I will be more understanding than he. I could behead you for spreading his lies, but instead, I will give you the second chance he never allowed me."

The screaming had died down. There were no more alien thoughts attacking Thomas's psyche, and he was released from his temporary hell. He looked up at Cain, who still had his hand upon his head. The ancient scars that covered the old vampire's body drew Thomas toward him. He felt all of Cain's pain as an empathetic connection emerged between the two of them.

"If there were one thing in this universe you wanted, what would it be?" Cain spoke with a care that only occurred between parents and their children.

Thomas did not stop to think about the question. The answer just poured from his mouth. "I ask him every day to rid Lilith of her pain."

"And he has not answered your prayers?" Cain looked down on the young man and shook his head slightly.

Thomas had intended to answer but felt such a connection with Cain at that moment, he just looked into his eyes. "You are the perfect example," Cain began. "You can ask for anything and you ask to help your fellow person. If that is not proof that vampires are just as virtuous as humans…" He trailed off for a moment, then said a few more words as he glided over to where Lilith was lying. "How could he punish such an honorable species of beings?"

Cain stood next to Lilith, allowing his huge body to nearly engulf hers. He bent at the waist and leaned in close to the motionless woman. His jaw seemed to dislocate as he sunk his teeth into her neck. It was the most graceful attack ever witnessed. Thomas's love seemed to have inspired Cain as he caressed the woman's arms while he devoured a small amount of her blood.

She lay perfectly still on the altar, but inside her body a thrashing from the change occurred. Her blood mingled with the vampire's venom which had entered her through the twelve small punctures in Lilith's neck. The blood surrendered to the venom, which, in turn, overtook all her vital organs. The condemnation from God controlled the clear venom and forced the body to submit its dependence on food and oxygen. Those enslavements were replaced by a reliance on blood. Her biology died as she became a creature of the night instead of a being of God.

Her outward appearance changed before Thomas's eyes. Her hair slicked with a shine unnatural to any being on the planet. Her skin lost its color and initially would remain grey, but as time would pass, there would be no avoiding its transition to opaqueness. Although she was still unconscious, she seemed to lose all of her premature aging. The beauty that Thomas saw in her skin disappeared as it tightened, removing all of her worries and wrinkles. Her bruises, scars, and broken bones all healed, fading the disgustingly mangled appearance she had.

Thomas jumped to his feet to get to Lilith's side, but before he could get across the floor, she sat straight up with her legs still stretched out in front of her. There was calmness to her movements that had been absent every time Thomas had seen her before. She turned her head about in both directions as if looking at the world from a new perspective, appearing astonished by simple structures and motions.

Thomas reached his love and knelt by her side. "Are you OK?" Her response would dictate his next chain of actions. While he was aware he had no chance in a physical altercation with Cain, if she were hurt, he would have to risk it.

She turned to him with a grin that had not shown itself in years. "I feel amazing. I don't know if I've ever felt this good." She turned sideways upon the altar, dangling her feet just inches above the old, tiled floor. Thomas looked at her and saw a child, a little girl in awe of the world. The smile on her face chased away all of Thomas's anger for Cain. There would be no battle that day. Lilith hopped to the ground with an optimistic bounce, grabbing both of Thomas's hands in the process and with pep in her voice she asked, "Did you do this for me?"

Thomas wanted desperately to take credit for her newfound elation. The brightness resonating from her now-colorless eyes tweaked Thomas's unnatural heart. Before he could formulate a response, Cain took command of the conversation. "The both of you prayed daily." Cain's voice had returned to its original aristocratic style with just enough force to feel paternal. "God never answered your prayers, but I am a merciful father."

Lilith seemed to not be paying any attention to the people around her as she wandered off, staring into the walls, exclaiming, "It is so bright in here." The statement was humorous to Jack and Thomas since there were no lights in the room. Everything was visible thanks to their night vision. The colors from the walls seemed to blend with the blues from the floor as her vampiric sight garnered control.

Cain smirked at the girl's discoveries. "The three of you should go now. Find refuge in the sewers until tomorrow night when you can emerge a new clan of three, the first new clan in fifty years." Cain walked off the platform and down between the subway rails, but as he disappeared into the darkness he sent Thomas a telepathic message.

Stay away from the police and the church. This is your second and final gamble. The words stuck to the back of Thomas's skull just as an annoying song had so many times in the past.

Thomas watched as Cain faded from his vision, leaving him confused about the biblical man as well as his own destiny. He was unsure about his standing with God and what his purpose was in that world of darkness. The one thing he knew without a doubt, however, was he appreciated Cain's assistance to Lilith.

A grinding sound came from above which brought Thomas's attention back from the subway tunnel he was staring at. He looked up and saw Jack leap up the manhole out of the old subway station chasing after Lilith, who was intending to explore the world with her new senses. A chuckle bubbled up from Thomas's throat as he began to climb the ladder out of the room, knowing that keeping Lilith out of trouble during the daylight would pose a challenge that morning.

Known Vampiric Biology

Sensuality is a deep-rooted emotion of vampires. It is buried deep, but when it surfaces, it overpowers most other emotions.

Lilith Year 0 Day 3 AV

Lilith dropped the remains of her victim into the lake outside the city. Her first feeding as a vampire came just two nights after her change, and she felt alive. She felt more alive now than she ever did as a mortal; she had found her escape from pain.

The three vampires stood beneath the moon and watched their victims bob up and down in the lake as they slowly sank down to meet the many other victims Jack had thrown there in the past.

Lilith had a crash course in vampires over the previous two days. Her mind was now filled to the brim with rules and myths about her new life as a dark entity of the undead. She could not turn into a bat or mist, and she could not be in the sunlight, although that would not kill her. She realized at the sunrise the first morning that it was painful. She could take a stake to the chest, she could eat garlic, she had to drink blood, but she must avoid severing her limbs at all costs. She tried her best to keep tabs on all of the things she had been taught, but with the intense police security around the city, her abilities were not the prime worry.

After Thomas's stunt over the courthouse, the authorities were on high alert in an attempt to find the flying man. Cain had gone into a deeper hiding than normal since Thomas and Jack's trail of destruction led the police directly to his lair. The authorities had searched the entire abandoned subway system and the city had sent workers in to gut it, trying to utilize the spare parts of the track and décor of the stations.

Father Timeus had closed his doors to the homeless, not that it was a big loss for the city since Thomas and Lilith were the only people who regularly made use of the building. Thomas had considered going back and talking to the priest. He considered the risk of having the cops turned loose on him as fairly acceptable, but every time he neared the church, Cain seemed to linger in the back of his mind, warning him not to go inside.

So, the three had hid the past two nights in a cemetery. An old tomb near the back of the graveyard was their current home. It stood by the short chain-link fence, hidden by the overgrown weeds of the oldest part of the burial ground. A couple of crows tended to watch over the tomb while the three escaped the torture of daylight, listening to their conversations and watching for vandals who may let the cruel light of day into the vampire's hiding spot.

Regardless of the security they had to avoid, the three

of them had enjoyed a great couple of days. Lilith broke out in a full sprint, engaging the boys in an impromptu footrace. Racing had quickly become Lilith's favorite pastime, realizing speeds that she had never imagined on foot while in no way creating any exhaustion to her system.

Pouncing over trees on their way back to the road, Lilith was quite a distance in the lead. Jack, always enjoying a challenge, increased his speed and reached the street back to town shortly after Lilith did. Thomas tried to keep up with the two of them as he had over the past couple of days, but ever since his anger vanished, he could not seem to achieve the intense speeds he had during his night of chaos.

Thomas watched the other two in the distance as they bounded over trees and nearly disappeared into the city. He maintained a mediocre pace, knowing that he had no chance to beat either of them. He flew by cars and the occasional pedestrian, still moving at speeds that humans could not possibly achieve. Thomas assumed the destination was the cemetery, so he turned down a street and leapt onto a grocery store near where he was headed. Two steps on the roof and he was about to jump back to the ground when Lilith jumped out of a tree directly in front of him.

"Boo!" she said as she flew in front of his face, leaving a resounding echo in the surrounding area, causing Thomas to flinch and lose his balance, falling from the grocery store roof to the hardened ground below.

He landed with a solid thud and whined as he hit, as if he could feel the impact. "What was that for? You are so mean." The end of his sentence ran on as if the word "mean" had eight or nine syllables, just the way a five year old might whine.

Lilith hopped to the ground, laughing and flaunting her sharp teeth. "Oh, you big baby. Come here and I'll lick your wounds." She swayed her hips side to side, trying to entice Thomas as she had done on a fairly constant basis recently.

Thomas released a smile that would have lit up Lilith's world had light not been her greatest enemy. He got to his feet and took her by the waist, pulling her anorexic frame into his more healthy looking structure.

"Maybe Jack will get out of the bedroom for a little bit and give us some alone time." Of course, that would not be an issue. Jack tried to say no the night before, but that was not going to stop the two lovers' amorous side, so he left the small tomb to keep his nausea down.

When they reached the tomb, Jack stepped out to let the two get the lust out of their system. Inside the darkened grave, Thomas looked at Lilith and ignored their earlier sexual tension. "How do you run so fast?" He was speaking out of true curiosity.

Lilith refused to let him end the sexual playfulness and responded, "I am smaller and I have less wind resistance." She slipped out of her clothes as she spoke, slowly dragging her hand across her chest as if she were rubbing lotion into her skin. "Now come here, Mr. Dead Man."

The two embraced in a sensual caress of passion as Lilith removed Thomas's clothing. It was a macabre dance, which included dirty sexual desire, ripping of flesh, and a true connection that had rarely been experienced by the living or the not. After their lusty romp in the tomb, the two of them lay there twisted from their debauchery, with wounds healing around each other's invading fingers in the most sensual of actions. They lay on the dirt next to each other, holding one another while they basked in the perfection of their sin.

The corpses had been pushed to the sides of the small room to make space for their living quarters. The pitch-black room was as bright as day to them. When the stone door closing them in moved to the side and Jack entered, witnessing the two young vampires stark-naked with bits of earth stuck to their bodies, it made him want to exit immediately, but it was not an option. He just threw his hands into the air in disgust of their appearance.

"I hate to interrupt, but it seems as though the police are searching our graveyard." Jack was on his hands and knees frantically digging into the ground.

"OK, I guess we will have to take them if they check our tomb." Thomas had begun to redress himself as Lilith just lay on the dirt, admiring her lover's body.

Jack looked up at Thomas with a surprised glare. "Aren't we trying to stay hidden so they think you left town or something?"

"Well, what option do we have? We are inside this tiny tomb."

"Just pull those coffins back to the center of the room." Jack paused, looking over at Lilith still sans all of her clothes and nibbling on her finger. "And put some clothes on!" Jack was constantly astounded by Lilith's transformation. From Thomas's early descriptions of the woman, she was meek and shy, but her change had brought out a mischievous troublemaker.

The police crept through the cemetery, holding their breath from the spooky terror that had followed them inside the gate. The ground seemed to crack beneath their weight, but they trudged on, guns pulled, waiting for a zombie to pop out of the ground.

"What are we doing here? There is no such thing as flying men!" a short officer who had worked on many of the embalming killer's cases said, realizing the absurdity of their current activity.

The larger cop continued to walk cautiously with his gun pointed forward. "You didn't see that guy. He was flying over the square! I did not see a helicopter or anything to hold him up. I never believed in ghosts or nothing before but… What was that?" The large cop turned toward a small tomb left in the corner of the cemetery.

"It was that stupid bird scratching at a headstone or something. Seriously, let's get out of here and solve some real crimes. It's not like we're some kind of ghost hunters or something." The short cop had put his gun back in its holster. "I got my kid's play to worry about tonight. I can't be spending all this time in a graveyard."

The taller cop was approaching the tomb, expecting to shoot something undead when he opened the door.

The short cop continued his rant. "For Christ's sake, there is no one here! Let's go grab some coffee or something, man."

The tall cop pushed with all of his strength, the door to the tomb moved only the slightest bit, but it was enough to put the flashlight in the tomb and look around for someone. There was nothing but a couple of coffins. The tall cop breathed a sigh of relief and shouted back to his partner, "All right, let's get out of here."

There was a real sense of liberation with both men as, regardless of their actions, they both were extremely afraid of a zombie attack.

Thomas shot up, throwing the coffin to the ceiling of the tomb, smashing it into hundreds of tiny splinters and sending down the old corpse onto his head. He did not like hiding half-buried under a coffin, but it was best for their situation. It would be ideal if the authorities eventually gave up so he could live in the night in peace.

After moving the remaining coffin back to the side, they all lay in the tomb, staring at the walls. The blandness of their tiny prison was a detriment to modern architecture. Civilizations of the past had always adorned the inside of tombs and burials, but the modern decorum was just flat walls and ceiling, no pictures, no treasures, a complete disregard for the dead.

Lilith stared off into nothingness, knowing that she had hours before the sun retreated down past the skyline. She felt herself changing again. She had gone days without thinking about anything that she had been worrying about for the last few years. Having been changed for a couple of days now, her thoughts seemed to drift back to her issues over Amon. She began her barrage of questions to the boys, which had become her ritual over the last couple of days as soon as they settled in for the day. "I feel that the novelty is wearing off. I am not feeling as excited as I have been over the last couple of days."

Thomas took notice when Lilith said those words because he felt himself returning back to a desire to serve God. "That's odd. I kind of feel the same way. I was so elated the last two days, but now…"

Jack interrupted. "It's Cain. He has a way of pulling people out of their funks, but it wears off after a bit."

Lilith chimed back in, trying to keep her mind on her new life. "I still can't believe the thrills we have now. I have lived here my entire life and I have never seen half of the things I am experiencing now. Had either of you ever seen the inside of a tomb or hung from a skyscraper in the open air in your past life?" Thomas and Jack smiled as they shook their heads to silently encourage Lilith's monologue. "Can we travel?"

Jack, having been across most of the world, scratched at wooden pieces of the former coffin stuck to the ceiling of the tomb as he responded, "Sure, we can… anywhere you want to go."

"Paris? Australia? Japan?"

"You just have to sneak on a plane." He laughed to himself. "And let me tell you, riding on the wing of a plane is the most exhilarating activity you can do. It scares the passengers beyond belief." Jack hummed the Twilight Zone theme.

Lilith went on. "It's hard to not be happy about the whole vampire thing. We get to live an entire life, plus I have night vision, speed, stealth…" She went on about the different abilities she had, sounding like she was taking role call of her powers.

Thomas turned to his side, caressing her thigh with his fingertips, rubbing it up and down, skin on skin, with her dress pulled up just a bit. He was relaxed and loving the feel of Lilith's skin as he interrupted her, trying to end her list of capabilities. "We have every chance to experience anything anyone could ever want with no time table and no physical danger to worry about."

"The only thing we miss out on is the afterlife," Jack mumbled to himself, letting a fleeting thought of Thomas's former mission cross the transom of his mind.

Jack continued to scrape the ceiling, Thomas let his hand glide just slightly higher up Lilith's thigh, but Lilith halted all movements. She sat completely frozen with a painful realization plastered upon her face. Her façade of terror went unnoticed by the boys as they continued to jest about their possibilities in the world.

Jack began to list ridiculous activities they could do. "Dive off a skyscraper."

Thomas retorted back, "Parachute with no chute."

"Run out on the field at a baseball game."

"Run out on the dirt at a rodeo."

"Run out on the battlefield in the middle of war!"

"How about hitching a ride into space?"

Lilith curled into a ball, not paying any attention to what the guys had been joking about. Thomas, finally noticing Lilith's distress, hushed Jack, bringing his attention to the one of their clan who had fallen silent.

He picked up Lilith's hand and looked at her with a desire to do nothing but reverse her sadness. She looked back at him with her old dead eyes and let her voice express her thoughts.

There was no emotion in her anymore, no cracking in her voice, just flatness. "I wanted only one thing for the last few years. And I thought that Cain had taken that pain away by turning me, but in the process, he destroyed my only true dream." She paused, expecting to choke back tears, but there were none. "I can't get to heaven. And I will never see my son again."

The epiphany was so distressing she punched the ground with all of her power. A shockwave went into the earth, creating a rumbling that was felt miles away. A crater formed where Lilith's hand had hit the ground, disturbing the structure of the tomb. Just a small adjustment to the crypt, but it unnerved Thomas and Jack.

Lilith stood up, hitting her head against the concrete roof of the tomb. She spoke, but it was mostly for her own benefit, trying to unravel the complications in her life. "I blinded myself. I lost sight of what mattered. I fell for someone, losing sight of the love for my son and God is punishing me for it. I had dedicated my life to Amon and my God, then I let lust get in the way. I am a heathen and a whore. I deserve nothing."

Thomas felt his hatred for Cain return as he watched someone who he thought was the most beautiful woman in the world crumble because of Cain's selfish actions. He pleaded with her to stop blaming herself. "It isn't you and it isn't God. Cain did this! He knew and he changed you anyway."

She did not listen to Thomas. Instead, she walked to the door of the tomb and threw it out into the graveyard. A blinding light filled the inside of the crypt, leaving Thomas and Jack trying to shield their faces from the sun's vicious attack. The slab that had kept the tomb closed was broken into the three pieces, which littered the ground a couple hundred feet away from the memorial itself.

The pain from the sun was not going to stop Lilith. She marched out into the illuminated yard in desperation to end her mental suffering. The pain she had felt for so many years could not come back. After having been happy for a few days, the possibility of returning to that cerebral hell was unfathomable.

Thomas and Jack were stunned at Lilith's determination and fled the tomb in an attempt to get her to return to the darkness. It was only steps outside when Thomas could no longer open his eyes, the sunlight was so intense. Jack fell to one knee ten feet into the excruciating glow of the fiery star. Neither of them could get near Lilith as she was standing on her feet in the center of the cemetery.

"Please, don't do this!" Thomas pleaded to his companion.

"I will not go through this again. I can't live without him." Lilith had fallen to her back as the pain was too much for her muscles to withstand. Lying on the ground, her arms straight out to her side and her body slightly damp from the prolonged state of the morning dew, the sunlight bore into her skin. The burning was felt deep within, as if she were being cooked from the inside out.

Thomas cried out to her as he dragged himself under the shade of a tree on the side of the burial ground. "Please come back. This is doing nothing but causing more pain!"

Lilith laughed a bit as her skin began to catch fire just around her orifices. She was insulted that Thomas thought he knew what pain was. He had never felt a loss like she did and until then, he had no right to decide what she should be doing. The flames grew as they licked her hair and clothes, her skin beginning to melt away.

"This is not pain. You don't know what pain is," she called back to him, refusing to give him any leeway. Realizing that she was physically hurting but was not dying, she grabbed a stick on the ground next to her.

Beyond the bubbling of her skin and the visible bones now coming through, she plunged the stick into her chest and punctured her useless heart. Having forgotten which vampire myths were real and which were tall tales, she tried to weep at her perpetual life. Of course, no tears came. She just lay in the sun, burning to a barely recognizable figure, accepting the torture of nature.

Jack had retreated back into the tomb and Thomas was curled into a ball under the shade of the tree, hoping that he would not burst into flames as well.

Lilith defied the odds and got to her half-melted feet and slowly limped back to the crypt where they had been staying. She grabbed Thomas on the way and dragged him into the small room with her. Jack grabbed one of the coffins and set it in the entrance to block the intruding sunlight.

Lilith, with a hunched back and staring at the earth, whispered to herself, "I can not die. A stake to the heart and nothing. Lying in sunlight, I am still alive." She ripped the branch out of her chest and the wound inched together instantaneously.

Jack was lying faceup in the dark box, recovering from their expedition into pain. "I told you already, there is only one way to kill a vampire. We can not survive a beheading, but even then, we are damned by God, so who's to say what happens to us after death?" Jack was exhausted and angry at Lilith for leading them into the sunlight.

Thomas spoke to himself, although it was heard by

all, "Jesus can save us."

Jack retorted, "You know that is impossible. Like Cain said, he is gone." He stood up, having to bend at the waist to fit in the room. Looking down at Lilith's chest, he saw her clothes were torn from the stab wound, but her chest was solid. The melting had subsided and the skin was regenerating with no scar. He felt no sympathy for the girl anymore. She had forced herself to be stuck in the rut she was in. "Stop trying to kill yourself. Your life force will not let you die. It will heal you regardless."

The three stayed in the tomb until the end of the day, but it was the last time they would do so. After that, the three of them would not be together again.

Jack's Diary

Although he is in my clan, I hope he dies.

Thomas Year 2 Day 126 AV

Thomas and Lilith stood inside of Thomas's former place of work. It was just as Thomas remembered it: full of despair, full of dust, and containing two corpses. These dead bodies were technically new additions, but it reminded him of a memory that he now reminisced over. The last night of his life when Jack came and birthed him into the ways of darkness was something he surprisingly cherished.

The two bodies were the most recent meal for Thomas and Lilith, both completely drained of blood and left on the floor to be discovered. Thomas had just called the police to report his own murder. Lilith stared down at the two former robbers and felt bad about how she was forced to take lives for her own health. How could she continue on like that when she knew just how hard it was to lose a family member? She cried inside for the families she just tore apart.

Thomas dropped a handwritten piece of paper on the chest of one of the men. He then grabbed Lilith's hand and they slowly walked out of the convenience store. They strolled down the street, walking by every memorable spot in the city. They both knew that this was the last night they would stay there. Thomas had plans to deal with Cain and that would either end his existence or he would leave town after he was done. The time was drawing near. It would not be long before Cain sought out Thomas for returning to his holy crusade.

There were still law enforcement officers crawling all over the city, but the two vampires had an easy time staying in the shadows and not bringing attention to themselves. They walked through the park, absorbing the beauty of nature snuggled inside the man-made creation of nature within the city. They passed the square, witnessing the monumental achievement of the courthouse. They passed through the neighborhoods, the poor ones and the rich ones, always staying in the shadows, not visible to anyone who happened to pass by.

Around the time that they passed by the library where Lilith had her eye-opening experience, she asked Thomas what was on the note. She was hoping it was a suicide note and that they could behead each other so she could leave the torment that was her life.

"It says that I was lost. The display they saw was a display created by Satan and it would be the last. That the people of this town should abide by the commandments, but it would be their decision. I am leaving town and they will never have to solve another of my murders again."

Thomas looked into Lilith's eyes which displayed no

emotion anymore. "It also mentions the lake where all of Jack's victims were left. For the families, you know?"

She knew. As she watched the city pass by her for the last time, she understood that he revealed the lake for her. He wanted to honor her loss by trying to bring closure to others who were missing their families.

Jack's Diary

I always feared the apocalypse, but now, I feel at home as it is upon us.

Thomas Year 2 Day 127 AV

After hours of walking, they came back to the church. It was just after midnight and together, they stood on top of the manhole cover which housed Cain, Thomas's immortal enemy. He wanted to look at the church as the house of God, but all he could see was Lilith's prison. She had spent years in that building, trying to find happiness and for a few more hours she would return.

He looked forward to their trek outside of the city, going across the country to spread the Word of God. Thomas took Lilith's hand, and together, they walked up to the front doors of the house of worship.

He pushed the door open and peered into the dark room. Their vampiric sight faded and they wandered into darkness, past the white judgmental walls, and into the worship hall. Chandeliers lit the huge room, creating a beautiful glow throughout the hall that made them both feel the love of God.

Thomas looked up to see Father Timeus walking toward the two of them. His face was full of sorrow and regret. He knew that the Lord had granted him his last chance at redemption. Lilith collapsed into a pew. Being back in the church brought back years of memories of grieving. She reverted back to her habits of praying, shaking from the sorrow.

The priest looked up at Thomas, torn from emotions. "You can't be here. The police have torn this place apart looking for something to lead them to you." He looked over at Lilith and saw her new pale skin, now showing more of her veins through the thin covering. He gasped in horror, as if the sight confirmed for him that Thomas was always a demon. He had turned Lilith, and together, they had come to avenge and end Timeus's miserable life.

"Father, we are sorry, but we have to be here. You should go to your office and pray. There is an evil on its way that you do not want to experience." Thomas did not want to force the priest to vacate his own church, but he felt there was no option. Cain would be there soon. He had to know they were in the church.

The priest lost all the color in his face, afraid he was about to face the ultimate evil. "The beast from the abyss?" Timeus could not believe it was happening.

Lilith looked up from her pew and apologized to the priest. She repented to him for her wrongdoing; she confessed her sins and begged for forgiveness. Timeus could not think straight. He blessed the girl and forgave her through habit, although she had nothing to truly be sorry for.

Thomas led Lilith past the priest and down the stairs. The old familiar stairs gave Thomas flashbacks of his last few years, of his desire to be with Lilith, of his connection to God. As they descended down into the darkness of the church, Lilith asked Thomas why she could not see, why she felt the pain of her son again, and why she could not hear the floors above.

Thomas had no good answers but said that he had decided a while back that inside the house of the Lord, they were once again creatures of God.

There was silence in the church. The priest had taken Thomas up on his advice and hid inside his office. Lilith lay downstairs waiting for Thomas to get her so they could live happily ever after, and Thomas knelt before the altar, looking at the darkened stained glass of the Pearly Gates. His mind had quieted, allowing him room to speak to God. He left his eyes open in case he was suddenly confronted by an angry biblical figure, but his hands were clasped together, fingers intertwined around one another.

He intended to pray to himself, but his mouth refused and he began to speak to the Lord aloud. "I am sorry." His voice bounced off the walls of the church, reverberating back toward his ears. "I was set adrift, and I lost sight of your guidance. Cain hijacked my mind. You know how he can be. You dealt with him once upon a time." Thomas rubbed his hands across the satin dressing that was draped across the altar.

"Please forgive my foray into the darkness. Please forgive my lack of character which did not tell me to ignore Cain. But it is not just me, please forgive Lilith as well. She was forced into the situation and did what came natural to her. She wants nothing more than to serve you and her son. And also please help Jack as he is a good man who has been convinced of certain things. Please send him the message of your holiness."

Thomas stood up, turning around to see the church from the vantage point of the priest during service. He raised both of his hands and held them out to the side. "Please bring an end to Cain's tyranny. There is a whole species of being that worships him because he has convinced them you turned your back on us. I know you still love all of your creations; please help us." He looked forward, taking in the calmness that the church tended to produce.

"Please send Cain to hell where he belongs. I want to ask that you allow Lilith, Jack, myself, and all the other vampires into your kingdom. Lilith is repentant for moving away from you. She understands that Christ is her savior. Please help us find the way back to your embrace." A vision of Jesus on the cross appeared before him.

His skin was browned from the sun, with burns upon his face and shoulders. He hung in an agonizing fashion as his blood dripped from the nails in his wrists. Hanging there naked, his body shriveled from dehydration, but there was no humiliation on his face. He was hanging in acceptance of his fate, something he willingly did for all of humanity.

Thomas opened his mouth to speak, but as he did, the apparition raised its head and stared at Thomas with compassion in his gaze that warmed him beyond compare. The image of Jesus of Nazareth spoke to Thomas through his thoughts. *It is my body and blood I have given so you can be free.*

Thomas heard the words and the phantom Christ faded into the pews behind him. He hit the wooden floor with his knees as he was so moved by the image of Christ sacrificing his physical body for Thomas's spiritual one. He screamed out to God, "I will honor you. I will spread your gospel. I will not turn a soul to evil."

He returned to his feet and walked back behind the altar again with his arms out to his sides. He was being led by the Holy Spirit and had no control over his movements. "Pater noster, qui es in caelis." He did not know what he said. The words just ran out of his mouth. His arms raised above his head meeting in a steeple and then lowering down in front of his chest. "Sanctificetur Nomen Tuum." His hands separated as if he were opening a book. "Adveniat Regnum Tuum." He bowed to both of his sides. "Fiat voluntas Tua." He touched his tongue with the tips of his fingers. "Sicut in caelo, et in terra." Thomas bent forward to pick up an imaginary cup when the doors at the back of the church flew open, slamming into the walls, sending a mind-numbing boom across the room.

Cain stood there in the doorway staring at Thomas who had snapped out of his holy interpretive dance. Cain spoke with the force of a stampede of elephants. "The Lord's Prayer and in Latin, no less. I told you to stay out of this church!" He took long, deliberate steps toward the altar. "But you just couldn't stay away from God's plan. You must not want mercy!"

Thomas walked around the edge of the altar to look Cain directly in his eyes. He knew how powerless he was against the ancient man, but felt this was his destiny. Whether he was to die at the hands of the man or he was to end the tyranny, he knew what he must do. Thomas raised his lips to show his razor-sharp teeth, an alpha male act that would do nothing to shake Cain's confidence.

"I was mistaken. I thought I was here to serve the Lord and spread the gospel, but that was not it. I was brought here and turned into a vampire to end your tyranny. I am here to help the vampire clan to find God and return home to his kingdom." Thomas said these things with malice in his voice.

"You only exist because of me! You have brought forth your own destruction. You can not stand up to me as I am a god among immortals!"

At this moment, the priest ran out of his office, hearing the commotion. The scene he saw displayed before him tore the breath out of his lungs. There was no communication between the priest and Thomas, but he knew instinctively who stood before him. He felt the tragedy of Cain's murder of his brother and Timeus wanted to hide from this unholy man. The old priest sprinted from his door to behind the altar, kneeling down with his head on the floor, immediately in deep prayer. "Ephpheta, quod est, Adaperire. In odorem suavitatis. Tu autem effugare, diabole; appropinquabit enim judicium Dei." The words were frothing at the mouth of the holy man when Cain began a maniacal laughter.

"It is no use, old man! Your exorcism will do nothing to me. I may have to follow God's law in this building, but your prayer is nothing but a children's story," he spat. Cain turned back to Thomas.

"I have returned to God. I will spend eternity preaching to vampires. Lilith will spend eternity waiting for Christ to return so she can see her son again. And you can spend eternity in hell for all I care," Thomas screamed at Cain, spittle flying as his emotions overtook his actions.

Cain rubbed his clear skinned chin, moving his jaw bone to each side as he thought about Thomas's insults. The bone itself appeared to absorb some of the gory flesh that churned while Cain rubbed his skin. He leaned over, putting his nose within an inch of Thomas's. As Cain opened his mouth to speak, Thomas could smell the stench of death, rot, and feces coming out of it.

"You can do whatever you want. You can say whatever you want, but it doesn't change the fact that God hates you! He hates all of us. Remember, I gave you your second chance and you threw it away. I can't have you here anymore, a thorn in my side. You threaten my existence, so you end here." Cain opened his mouth to bare his teeth, his pupils transforming to vertical slits like those of a cat.

"It's too bad you chose to come here. You could have gone away anywhere. If we were on the street this would be quick and painless, but you chose the house of the scumbag. And you must follow his laws in here. There will be pain and suffering because that is how he likes it. Remember, everything hurts in God's house!"

Cain's teeth sank deep into Thomas's shoulder. The moment they made contact with his skin it felt like the stinging of a thousand hornets. The old man's breath almost soothed the pain, until he inhaled, which sent the burn down into Thomas's arm, throughout his hand and back to the wound. As Cain pulled back, taking some of Thomas's flesh with him in his teeth, the entire arm throbbed with near-convulsive strength.

Cain grabbed the boy by the scruff of his neck and threw him back toward the entrance of the church. He did not have his vampiric super strength inside the church, but his large frame wielded a fair amount of power anyway.

Thomas was off balance, jogging toward the doors in an attempt to regain his control. He hit the basin with the holy water. The blessed liquid spilt out onto the floor, flowing quickly under the pews to the side of the hall. The rushing water flowed over Cain's feet, burning the skin of his condemned body. He hopped onto one of the pews to avoid more burning from the water.

Thomas, believing that this was his last stand, grabbed his shoulder and pressed through the pain. He charged down the center aisle of the church heading toward the stone altar. As he passed, Cain leapt from the pew and tackled him to the ground. The impact with the floor caused some of Thomas's clear vampire venom to splatter from his wound and across the old wood. He tried to get to his feet, but Cain grabbed the boy by his waist and with all the speed the old vampire could muster, slammed Thomas into the side of one of the pews.

His ribs crushed under the unyielding wood and the brute force of the man. He was doubled over in pain. Only his refusal to give in to evil allowed him to continue. He got to his hands and knees atop the seat of the pew, clear fluid dripping from the gash in his shoulder and saliva from his mouth.

Cain, having returned to his feet, smiled at the torment his prey was receiving while the body fluids slowly made their way across the wooden pew, sinking into the framework, a permanent reminder of their altercation. With a monstrous chuckle, Cain clasped his hands together and lowered them across Thomas's back, cracking at least one vertebra in the process.

Thomas flipped to his back, sending shots of pain down his spine, kicking and scratching at the pew, trying to escape from Cain's advances. As Cain approached, Thomas lifted his foot with all his might, kicking the old man in the temple. The neck of his enemy snapped to the side from the abrupt kick to the face, but his head swiveled back around with a malevolent smile that showcased his yellowed grill.

There was another encroachment and Thomas landed a punch to the gut. Cain returned quickly, just in time for another kick, this time to the groin. Nothing was slowing Cain and after every attack from Thomas, he was right there, inches away from his prey, nipping at his heels.

Thomas knew that there was no escape, so he turned to the only source of protection he could find. To his side tucked into a corner of the pew was the Holy Bible. Thomas snatched it from its hiding place and held it over his face, hoping that God would combat Cain for him.

Cain stood up straight with his burned feet still tingling at the touch of the rigid wooden floor. He looked down on Thomas and laughed as if he were just let in on an inside joke. "I told you he hates you. And now you think the papers within his book of lies are going to save you?" He continued his laughter as he struck the book in Thomas's hands and knocked it across the room. With Thomas defenseless, he pummeled him in the jaw, forcing it out of socket.

The pain pounding in Thomas's body was nearly unbearable as the venom dripped from his wounds. Spitting up fluids from the crack in his jaw, Thomas tried to crawl away, but his shoulder was unusable. He stumbled as he crawled, military style, across the pew, losing his balance and falling to the floor. His head slammed against the hard wood floor, forcing a knock to scream across the room.

Cain looked down on the boy and lifted a foot to smash his skull in, but Thomas managed a kick to the shin. Cain was caught off guard by the swift strike, but found it utterly sad. He allowed a guffaw to spill out of his throat as he watched Thomas writhe on the ground trying to escape.

"Why are you even trying?" Cain posed the question to the battered boy dragging himself across the floor. "After thousands of years and thousands of rogue vampires who have all tested me and fallen, you believe it will be you who does me in?" Cain turned his back on the boy, trying to give him a sporting chance. A good time to go get the priest, Cain thought.

"You have been a vampire for a couple of years and you are nothing compared to my telepathy. You don't stand a chance against my sheer size." Cain was about to step around the altar to grab Father Timeus when he heard a crashing come from behind him.

He turned around to see Thomas hanging halfway out of a broken window on the side of the building. Cain turned back and sprinted, trying to get to the boy before he climbed back into the church, but he was too late. Thomas had quickly gone outside of the church where his body was not a creature of the Lord, where he did not have to follow God's laws, and he began to heal his injuries. He put both feet on the church floor, feeling like a whole person again just in time to see Cain charging him with a shoulder block. The hymnal Thomas used to break the window worked well as a bat also. He smashed the thick book into the skull of Cain, dislodging him from his locked-in target of Thomas's gut.

The force of the blow pushed Cain to the side, where he smashed his face into the brick wall, stunning him for a few moments. He clutched his head as he tried to get the feeling of a flattened skull out of his mind. Thomas reached to the window where he acquired a loose piece of glass the size of his arm. The shard was clear and in the shape of an icicle. The edges gleamed in the candlelight of the church, threatening both men with its razor edge.

Cain, having regained his mental clarity, clutched his fist in preparation to pound Thomas's ribs, but before he could take aim, the large piece of glass was shoved into his knee. The glass forced the kneecap over to the side and severed the muscles and tendons within. Cain fell to the ground, grasping at his leg, which was useless with its unattached muscles. Thomas still had a large gash missing out of his shoulder and with Cain down from his knee, he felt it was the time to lean out the window and repair it.

Cain seized the opportunity to shove Thomas out of the church and onto the grass, landing on his head, but the soreness evaporated as the outside air and the moon finished regenerating his body. When he looked back inside the church, he saw Cain smiling with revenge, trying to drag his body out of the shattered window. Thomas panicked. He knew he stood no chance against Cain once they were outside the Lord's house, but he was not in a position to knock him back into the church quickly enough. His life flashed before his eyes. His regrets piled up and his wishes died in an instant.

Just as Cain had a foot outside of the building and his skin re-grew over the burns from the holy water, Lilith tackled him from the side and forced his leg back into the church.

Thomas regrouped and jumped back in through the window. The force of Lilith's attack slammed Cain into the side of a pew, twisting his neck and forcing the large shard of glass out of his knee. Lilith walked over to the old vampire who was cradling his wounds.

"You claimed to have given me eternal life, but all you did was steal the only dream I had in this world." She stood above him prepared to stomp on his knee to keep him down. As she raised her foot, Cain swiveled his position and shoved the huge glass splinter into Lilith's abdomen. The glass entered her lower stomach at an upward angle, finding its way all the way up behind her ribs and near the base of her throat. She fell backwards, landing hard on the wooden floor, flailing her arms and legs about in pain, causing the floors to creak wildly.

Thomas, on the inside of the window, grabbed another shard of glass and made his way toward Cain. Passing by Lilith writhing in anguish, Thomas let fury overtake him as he approached Cain to end his tyranny once and for all.

Cain scrambled with his one good leg, but only got to the center aisle before Thomas was standing above him. Cain looked up at the chandeliers, seeing their dim flicker, knowing they would be one of the last sights he ever saw. He nodded at Thomas and closed his eyes in recognition of his defeat.

Thomas, without remorse, thrust the huge glass piece into the throat of his unholy opponent, stopping at the spinal cord, which he could not break through. Cain lay perfectly still, absorbing the torture, determined to die with dignity. Thomas bent down and retrieved the Holy Bible that Cain had knocked across the room earlier. He grasped the book with both hands and lifted it over his head. As the tome came striking down on the glass protruding from Cain's throat, the old vampire mouthed the words "thank you" to Thomas.

The Bible hit the end of the glass and forced it through the bones that were holding Cain's head on. The ancient skull rolled lopsided away from its former body, which had finally gone completely limp.

The spirits and the church itself rejoiced as Thomas could hear the angels singing his praises for vanquishing the evil Cain. The body lay on the old floor of the church, oozing its venom from its open wound, mixing with the holy water that sat stagnant in the room.

There was a moment of realization when Thomas understood that he had rid the world of an evil force which had been plaguing the earth for centuries. He wanted there to be a religious epiphany that followed, something that could rival his vision of Christ or his speaking in tongues earlier, but nothing happened. It was as if God stepped back once he had done his duty.

Thomas looked up at the Pearly Gates, which were still dark with night shining in and allowed a river of calm flow through his veins. He was safe from Cain. Now, he and Lilith could leave town to spread the Word of God to the vampire community. He looked back over his shoulder to see Lilith still on the floor clutching at the glass impaled in her stomach.

She let out a moan that only the priest had heard before. It was the sound of her giving up on life and trying to let death take her away. Timeus came out from behind the altar to see Thomas lifting Lilith up with his arms under her shoulders. Getting to her feet, the clear liquid of her vampiric internal organs splattered on the wood below, leaving a dark trail.

Thomas was about to pull the glass out when the priest warned him not to. "The wound is too large. There won't be anything holding in her entrails." He tried to soften the warning, but it was still a powerful blow to Thomas.

"It's fine. Let's just get outside where she can heal." Thomas was avoiding the reality that he knew was there, but he just wanted to live happily ever after.

Lilith looked over at Thomas, brushing his cheek with her hand. She spoke as softly as her vocal chords would let her. "No. I love you, but I cannot go on anymore." She looked at Father Timeus with relief in her eyes and gave him a smile.

There was no question between the two of them. They both understood what needed to happen.

The priest walked gingerly by the corpse of Cain, not removing his eyes from the body just in case it jumped up to attack him. As he went to the altar and rummaged around its drawers he asked one simple question. "You have been baptized?" There was a silent nod while Lilith focused on dealing with the pain.

Thomas helped Lilith over to the altar where she kneeled on the ground with the glass pressed against her legs keeping her genuflect. Her head draped down toward the floor with her old posture trying to return.

Thomas sat down in a pew and gritted his teeth as he watched Lilith perform her last prayers.

The priest stood behind the altar, holding a pressed bread wafer over his head. He began the prayer of the Holy Communion, bringing the wafer down to his chest and breaking it in half. Thomas watched the ritual as the priest recited the prayer and did the exact routine Thomas had done alone in the church speaking in tongues before Cain appeared. God had spoken through him, telling him to take communion, but he did not understand the significance until that moment.

The priest said his lines and Lilith responded when she was supposed to. After minutes of scripture and prayers, the priest approached Lilith. Before he gave her the bread, she prayed aloud. "Lord, please forgive my sins. I have tried to live life in the light of your love, to worship and honor you, to serve and live by your words. Amen."

Father Timeus placed the wafer on her tongue and

said, "The body of Christ, the bread of heaven." He turned back to the altar where he picked up the goblet of wine and upon tipping the drink into her mouth he stated, "The blood of Christ, the cup of salvation."

Both Timeus and Thomas were astounded at the changes that suddenly took place. With Lilith willingly accepting Christ into her body in the form of communion, the condemnation of her vampirism lifted. Her hair dulled out, starting at the scalp and dried down the strands to the end of her hair. Her color flushed back into her face with a visible plumping as the skin filled with the thick redness of her blood. Her eyes returned to their original pigmentation and her teeth dulled down as if they were watching a time-lapse video. But the touch of Christ did not stop with Lilith, the first vampire to be saved, the event returned a small amount of humanity to all of vampire kind. Thomas looked on with new pigmentation in his eyes, glowing a magnificent red, as he gazed at the miracle in front of him.

The transformation back to a human was a miraculous sight which could only have been achieved through divine intervention, which was the reversal of thousands of years of betrayal. The pain Lilith had been feeling did not fade. It intensified as she leaned back and grasped the glass shard with both hands. She pulled down on the glass and slid it out of her stomach.

Her face contorted in pain as her organs were left with gashes that were not survivable. She fell back with a smack of her head on the wood, gasping for breath as her body ejected her blood out into the church. In her dying moments, she stared into Thomas's eyes from her upside-down perspective and whispered, "I love you."

Thomas watched as his soul mate bled to death on the old church floorboards, leaving an everlasting stain to remind the world of their foray with evil and their return to Christ.

Father Timeus looked to the ceiling and spoke. He was part speaking to Thomas, part speaking to himself, and part speaking to all the spirits and angels in the world. "We look to the Bible for the Word of God, but we forget that he shows us wisdom throughout our existence as well. She accepted Christ as her savior and took Jesus into her heart, so he took her home."

Known Vampiric Biology

Addendum: Vampires have a reprieve in the form of communion.

Thomas Year 2 Day 156 AV

Jack turned to Thomas, excited that the killing for sustenance was over. Thomas had fully adopted the feeding-off-of-the-dead technique that Jack finally got to show him. It was not as invigorating, but they both were trying to live a more respectable life and that included not murdering, even if it were for food.

As they walked down the road in the middle of the night, Thomas wondered what it would be like when they found a vampire. He hoped there would be no repeats of what happened with Cain, but after defeating the oldest of all vampires, he figured he was ready. Traveling across the country was a new adventure for Thomas. It may have been old hat for Jack, but searching for vampires to spread the Word of God was not.

After Cain was beheaded, Jack was overly joyous to help Thomas in letting others of his kind learn about God and their option to move on to the kingdom of heaven. The relief on Jack's face once he found out about Cain's end shocked Thomas since he seemed so antireligion beforehand, but the idea of living happily for eternity was a better future outlook for Jack than serving Cain's desires.

Jack looked straight ahead as he walked. "Thomas, I think there is an old clan in this town."

Thomas did not know how he knew, but he figured someone who has been around as long Jack may have developed a few more tricks than he had. "OK, you think we are going to meet any resistance here?"

"No, the places we need to worry about are the ones with the really old vampires. You know, the ones who have become the elders now that Cain is gone." Jack turned off the road and headed straight into the woods. "Most of these guys aren't going to be upset about Cain. And I think most of them would give up their immortal life on earth for an eternity above."

The idea made Thomas smile. There was nothing in the world he wanted more than to meet Lilith in heaven, but he needed to make sure the Word was spreading. He did not want other vampires to spend forever roaming Nod when they could be saved.

"Thomas?" Jack asked for his attention as they came upon an old shack in the woods with blacked-out windows. "What do you think happened to Cain? I mean, his soul was not saved, he refused the light of God, but he's dead, right?"

Thomas had pondered over this a few times since he killed the elder. "I don't know. Maybe he's in hell. Maybe he is still in his body and is just stuck somewhere." His words could not have been more true.

Cain still existed inside his decapitated body. His body was beyond repair and he could do nothing but exist. He wondered from time to time if his body would decompose after enough time without blood and if so, what would be of him then. It was a good question, but it would take decades, if not centuries or eons, to find out.

If you enjoyed this book or would like to support me, please consider leaving a rating or review. It really helps me out as well as those looking for something to read.

Reviews or ratings at

Amazon.com

Goodreads.com

Shepherd.com

Bn.com

Or where ever you buy or talk about books

Just look for

Richard W. Kelly

Fantasy Casting

Something I like to do is fantasy cast my books into movies. I've been doing it on my website for years. Meenduk.com, cheap plug… I think it is a fun activity and I would like include it in all my books. Since this one was written in 2010, I had a very different cast picked out than I would today. Realizing that, I am going to include my 2010 and 2024 picks for the characters in Testament

Thomas - I initially saw this being played by Andrew Garfield. I just needed someone who could be sullen and quiet. A contemplator of sorts. Nowadays I think I would cast Ethan Cutkosky. I feel that a lot of his work in Shameless is highlighted by his body and facial reactions which I what I feel Thomas needs.

Lilith - I wanted this to be Anne Hathaway. I think that is because I am big fan of hers and it felt like something she hadn't done. It always had to be someone who could dwell in depression and almost live in a subservient manner with hopes of an end. Today, I think that Brigette Lundy-Paine fits the bill. The few things I've seen her in really impress me and she is physically what I envisioned for Lilith.

Jack - In my head this was Neil Patrick Harris. I think that may still be the same today. Jack was an adult that was a child. Maybe not child as much as a teenager. Someone stuck in early adulthood that still was passionate about being young and causing trouble. Neil has a tendency to do this by skirting the line between comedy and drama, he is still my thought of Jack. But watching Ted Lasso the other day I realized that Phil Dunster who plays Jamie Tartt also finds that line between adult and child. I think he would have to be my modern -day pick.

Father Timeus - I initially thought this should be Steve Martin. I love everything that man does. To me I felt that his dramatic work in the Spanish Prisoner and Shop Girl showed how versatile he was. Today, I feel that the character needs someone who can truly show fear. Someone that can fake leadership behind a fear of the world. Ideally in today's world I would want to see Hugh Jackman in this role. He may be a bit too forward, but some of the faces of anguish I've seen him make scream this role to me.

Cain - As much as I think someone like The Rock is the right build for the character, I've always seen some kind of CGI assisted Stanley Tucci in this role. He has the power and passion behind him that this character needs. I know he doesn't look the part, but I think he would be the only perfect fit. He has to be serious, debonair, persuasive, and more than anything else he has to be gut wrenchingly believable in his personal feelings about God and humanity. I am not a casting director, but from all the movies I've seen in all the years I've been alive, Stanley Tucci is the perfect pick for the character of Cain.

A Note from the Author

This was my first novel. I wrote it in 2009 and 2010. I wanted to write a book before I was 30. I had always dreamed of being an author. I have books and comics that I wrote from the time I could put words on paper.

So, achieving this goal was a big moment for me. Of course, I thought that once I had a book, I would sell a bunch and be on my way to life as a paid author. But, similar to the degree I got, writing a book is far from a guarantee that you will be successful. I now have twelve books on the market and each one is a struggle to sell. I have a few fans that buy each one and I appreciate them more than they can realize.

I still have the dream, but now I realize that putting out these books is largely a necessity for me to keep sane. I have these stories that bounce around in my head for years. And sometimes I just need to get them out.

This one started as an idea for a comic book back in 2002. It was about a druggie that is thrown into a bathtub of LSD and then bitten by a vampire. In his drugged out mind he sees that vampire as an angel and believes that he is a messenger of God. We only got through a few pages although there were plans for two issues. In the end the workload was not evenly distributed. Writing is much quicker and easier than the art.

The novel originally was going down the same route, but the creative process pushed the story into a more metaphoric version of the same thing. This tends to happen when stories evolve over a decade or so.

I still love the idea, the comic book and the novel even if they all are a bit separate from one another now.

So, thank you for reading. Thank you for supporting me. And I hope you will join me for whatever comes next.

A Preview of the next tale

My next novel was a young adult fantasy. It was my first attempt to make something a bit more mainstream. It has to do with the supernatural and the military and a confused kid in high school. But rather than ruin any of the surprises I'll just put the first chapter here at the end of Testament.

It is a bit of a departure from my religious vampire horror story, but those of you who have read more of my work understand that I don't write one genre. I like to tell stories of all types in the same way that I read books in different genres, watch television and movies in different genres, and play video games of different genres.

Either way. Please give The Psi-Chotic Adventures of Drew Darby a try here with the first chapter.

ONE

SOLITARY CONFINEMENT, PLEASE

The engine revved with humiliation as Drew steered toward his new place of employment. The bright greens and yellows of his HappyLand employees' shirt mocked his sixteen-year-old brain with the unwanted reality that he was who he did not want to be.

A green light released him from his neighborhood drawing him ever closer to the ridicule that was likely to accompany his first day on the new job. His foot let up on the gas and shifted over to the brake pedal of his ten-year-old car. He drove the decade old rusted out hatchback every day to his high school where he lugged a huge tuba in and out of the small car and into the band hall where he helped the band director police the halls and snitch on his fellow students who were breaking rules. He sported old fashioned pilot glasses that came down below his cheek bones magnifying the blemishes on his face. He even let his hair hang shaggy and in need of a trim while leaving a receding hairline already noticeable at his young age. All these things and being employed by HappyLand left his stomach twisting with anticipation of the humility.

He drove his beloved vehicle into a left turn lane and

stared out the side window at the hideous fast-food restaurant that matched his bright shirt glowing from the corners of his vision. The light flashed a green arrow. He stared at the building. The arrow turned yellow, then red. Honks came from behind him upset that he refused to go to work. A deep breath filled Drew's lungs and he turned back to the traffic light.

His eyes trained on the red circle, but the cartoon-colored restaurant mocked him from the periphery. When the green arrow came back Drew forced himself to press the gas pedal just enough to approach the store. Dark music played in his head as he slowly crept toward HappyLand. The soundtrack in his mind could have been appropriate for an approaching army of demons, but that would somehow seem less intimidating than the idea of being seen working for HappyLand.

Still barely rolling down the road, his car gently drove up the driveway into the parking lot. He instinctively parked in the back and let his head fall into his hands as he overdramatized his unfortunate place of employment.

His stomach filled with the uncomfortable carbonation of anticipation as he opened the car door and placed his black sneakers on the asphalt. Every step he took toward the door felt like a step toward the end of his social life or at least what was left of it. As the wind played with his unkempt hair, he scorned his parents for forcing him to take a job.

They saw his lack of friends as a weakness and making

him gain employment was their only solution. His pleas for a reprieve fell on deaf ears when his father called an old buddy who happened to own a franchise of the horrid HappyLand outside their neighborhood.

Drew had told them he was fine, that he did not need money, that many highly looked upon people were hermits, but it was no use. Apparently, his parents did not want to raise a monk or a serial killer and chained him to the prison that was a job.

Drew looked at the door not wanting to walk inside. It was a metaphor for an entry into a darker world. Or maybe it was an exit from his childhood. Either way he did not want to enter. He could see Mr. Harkins walking around with perfect posture in his sweat-stained Wal-Mart business attire. The pale blue tie swung around his thick neck reminding Drew that his new boss and his father's longtime friend was former military. The realization of just how horrifying his new militaristically disciplined career may be caused his knees to go weak.

Drew's balance went and he fell forward with his face and the glass echoing an ugly splat into the dining room. This caught the ear of Mr. Harkins who quickly trotted over to obtain his new employee.

The manager's military humor kicked in as he pushed the door open with enough force to toss Drew into the parking lot while he remarked, "Oh, gee, didn't see ya there young man."

Drew pulled himself to his feet refusing to look Mr.

Harkins in the eye. He walked with slunk shoulders past his new boss and into the headache-igniting dining room of HappyLand. The bright greens and yellows made Drew squint in agony, a feeling he never felt as a customer in the grease-filled death trap.

Mr. Harkins looked down on the boy, slightly disgusted with his lack of self-hygiene or at least self-respect for his fashion sense. "Report to the training room behind the kitchen. You are a bit early, sit in a chair and wait for your trainer to arrive." He turned on his heel to march back to the bathrooms leaving Drew to find the training room on his own.

He watched the ground as he walked past the cashier's counter and into the kitchen. Slipping on the greasy floor he kept his eyes on the ground to avoid meeting a gaze with anyone who was employed there. He knew that he was on the low end of the high school totem pole, but that did not mean he did not want to move up on that scale and working at HappyLand could do nothing but the opposite.

A deep voice came from Drew's right directing him to the training room which he mechanically wandered into. The floor went from a greasy slip and slide to dry rubber tiles being temporarily tarnished by his now filthy black sneakers. The room was very empty - a chair, a television and a few inspirational posters on the wall. Drew collapsed into the chair, exasperated with defeat.

He looked at the walls ready to give in and accept the misery that was now to be his life. He read the first inspirational poster trying to convince his sub-conscience to learn its lesson.

The first in the nice line of six inspirationals said, "Get up and get to work, NOW." Drew thought to himself, 'I don't feel motivated.' The accompanying picture was no help either, just an empty boat with a paddle lying inside.

The next said, "The job you deserve is this one." The picture was a smiling cartoon sheep knitting a sweater. Another feeling of self-worthlessness swept over him.

"Hell isn't punishment, it's just for failures." Above the slogan was a picture of an ugly bodybuilder type man that had so much of a fake tan that he looked orange. In it he was signing a last will and testament and he was oddly happy about it. Drew could not stop his disgust at how demented Mr. Harkins was.

"Out of desperation, unwavering dedication is born." This one had a picture of a man from the eyes up tapping his temple as if to say, "What an epiphany this is." There was an odd tattoo on the man's hand, looking somewhat like the Greek letter 'delta'.

"Of everything you want, you have this." Mr. Harkins was pictured above the somewhat inspirational line in full military garb with a very serious look on his face, but for some reason he had one eye opened wide while the other was noticeably closed.

Drew thought how much his new boss had fallen from the height of the military to being a lowly fast-food manager.

The last poster bore the image of two people on a roller coaster with a thought bubble above their heads saying "YipeeeeeeE!" The last e in the word was oddly capitalized. Drew wondered about the purpose of the capitalization as he read the line below. "Here is the rest of your life."

He leaned back in the chair looking at the line of posters, the big E in the last still perplexing him. Out of boredom he started to play with the posters, counting the number of words in each phrase, looking for repeating words, comparing the background colors of each…

But after a couple of coincidences, he noticed something that made his neck hair stand on end. The first word of each poster made a sentence he did not want to see. "Get the Hell out of here." He figured it to be coincidence, but it made him a bit nervous.

Unable to sit still he continued searching the signs for other hidden messages. He kept staring at the E.

He looked at the 'delta' in the fourth picture and couldn't help but focus on Mr. Harkins' eye in the fifth. His heart began to race as he put the letters together. Delta was the Greek letter for D. Eye. E. DIE. Drew's breathing began to pound his chest. His heart was racing faster than he could handle.

The rest of the posters began to make sense. There was an oar in the boat. A female sheep was a ewe. The orange man was signing a will. He put them all together. Oar ewe will D I E. Get the Hell out of here or you will die.

Drew was terrified. Forget coincidence he decided as

he sprang toward the door realizing there was no handle on the inside. The message made no sense, there was no reason for him to fear for his life, but it was no time for logic.

Drew took a few steps back into the room and charged the door with a shoulder block. He bounced off the steel door and fell to the ground, his head cracking against a hard rubber tile dislodging it from the ground. He picked up the tile instinctively wanting to return it to its place when he noticed the word wrong was written on the back of it accompanied by a small twenty-seven. He turned to his side and ripped up the tile next to it.

Another wrong with the number twenty-six. Over the intercom came a weasel-y little voice speaking directly to Drew. "I'll be in a minute, why don't you turn on the TV before we get started."

Drew tried to ignore his fears and turned on the television, telling himself he was crazy. The old television came on with a small electrical buzz in the background.

There was a man in a HappyLand hat talking about inspiration, but Drew could not focus. He kept looking at the tiles on the ground that he had pulled up. There were eight tiles from wall to wall in each direction making sixty-four tiles total. Counting from the front corner of the room they were tiles number fourteen and fifteen. Counting from another direction they were tiles ten and eighteen. Why were they labeled twenty-six and twenty-seven?

The television spoke in the background, "At HappyLand we help every customer. We pay attention to every word. If we are speaking to a customer, we count every smile. If we are cleaning, we clean every tile. If we are reporting, we pay attention to every column and every row. "

Drew continued to try to calm himself down by taking slow relaxed breaths while the television repeated the same line over and over. As his heart rate slowed, the words of the TV drilled into his skull as if he was having brain surgery. He began to chant the line.

"Every word", he paused. "Every Smile", another pause. "Every column, every row", then it hit him. The tile was not labeled twenty-seven it was column two row seven. His connection to the randomness of the situation pumped the adrenaline back into his veins.

He repeated things to himself again. Word. Smile. Column. Row. He turned back to the poster and counted words again. Forty-two. That can't be it. Six posters and each had seven words. So, seven was the column. He looked back at the posters looking for smiles. The sheep was smiling, the orange man, and the two coaster riders. Four.

He kicked the chair out of the way to get to tile seven four. Again, fearing for his life, he pawed at the rubber square yanking it out of the ground. As the tile came up, he could see a small red button sunken into the ground. Without hesitation he pressed the plastic circle and the door popped open.

A wave of relief flushed through Drew's body as he saw his freedom open to the kitchen. Until he saw Mr. Harkins step into the door frame. The large fit man stepped into the room closing the door behind him.

"Let me out of here! My dad knows where I am!" Drew screamed out through the crackling in his pubescent voice. His hand kept mashing the red button popping the door back open.

Mr. Harkins kept slamming the door each time it popped open. His jaw began to clench and his face reddened. "Drew. Stop hitting that button. NOW!"

"I don't know why you want to kill me, but…"

"I am not going to kill you." He took a step toward Drew, but had to retreat to close the door again. "I said stop it."

Drew just kept pressing the button as tears weld up in his eyes.

"You are safe. I need your help actually."

"What are you talking about?" The words came out in globs past the tears streaming down the boys cheeks.

"Pull yourself together! You are the first one to solve the puzzle. You are only the second one to notice it even exists."

This caught Drew off guard. Maybe he was safe after all. "Puzzle?"

"Yes, it is just a puzzle. We need to be able to identify those who can read between the lines of the universe."

Drew popped the door again. He was relaxing a bit, but still didn't trust Mr. Harkins. "Who is we?"

"The United States military."

www.ingramcontent.com/pod-product-compliance
Lightning Source LLC
Chambersburg PA
CBHW020107310726
48970CB00002B/519